THE POWER OF SONG

In loving memóry
of our mother and gandmother,
Evelyn Lieberman

Aaron, Rachel, Gayle, and David Smith

THE POWER OF SONG
And Other Sephardic Tales

∽

RITA ROTH

2007• 5767
Philadelphia

JPS is a nonprofit educational association and the oldest and foremost publisher of Judaica in English in North America. The mission of JPS is to enhance Jewish culture by promoting the dissemination of religious and secular works, in the United States and abroad, to all individuals and institutions interested in past and contemporary Jewish life.

The Jewish Publication Society
2100 Arch Street
Philadelphia, PA 19103
www.jewishpub.org
Manufactured in the United States of America

07 08 09 10 10 9 8 7 6 5 4 3 2 1

Design and composition by Alexa Ginsburg

Library of Congress Cataloging-in-Publication Data

Roth, Rita.
The power of song : and other Sephardic tales / Rita Roth. — 1st ed. p. cm.
   ISBN 978-0-8276-0844-3
   1. Sephardim—Folklore. 2. Jews—Spain—Folklore. 3. Jews—Portugal—Folklore. 4. Tales.
   I. Title.
   GR98.R646 2007
   398.2'089924--dc22

                         2007001886

JPS books are available at discounts for bulk purchases for reading groups, special sales, and fundraising purchases. Custom editions, including personalized covers, can be created in larger quantities for special needs. For more information, please contact us at marketing@jewishpub.org or at this address: 2100 Arch Street, Philadelphia, PA 19103.

CONTENTS

To my husband, Larry Poisner, for his constant support,
thoughtful feedback, and endearing patience

PREFACE

If one desires to look at the soul of a people, look at its folklore. The Rabbis of the Talmud advanced this thought by placing a great deal of importance upon *aggadah,* the term for both the legendary and the imaginative interpretation of the narratives of the TANAKH—the Jewish Bible.

Every people, from antiquity to the present, spins its own stories about life and death, courage and cowardice, good and evil, free choice and destiny, heroes and villains. The best-known themes of folklore are found in the literature of all ethnic groupings, albeit with many variations. Most of the tales by Hans Christian Andersen, a Dane, and the Brothers Grimm, who were German, may be found restructured and reimagined in the folklore of other peoples. Keen students of the genre pay special attention to variations of the stories. These variations almost always represent the outlook of the people in whose language the tales are told or written.

Rita Roth's work reflects industriousness and imagination. She has presented a fascinating collection of folktales with a good number of variations emphasizing changes in motifs prevalent among the Sephardic Jewish people. The Jews of *Sefarad* (Hebrew for the Iberian Peninsula) had a history of nearly 1,400 years in Spain. Between the 10th and the end of the 15th centuries, Hebrew poets, philosophers, diplomats, and philanthropists crafted a literary culture of the very highest merit. They were responsible for the "Golden Age" of Iberian Jewry. The 200,000 Jews who were victims of the Spanish Expulsion of 1492 carried this rich legacy with them. Much of the folklore incorporated in this volume had its origins in Spain.

The perceptive reader can learn much about the Jewish soul by noting the omissions from and additions to the standard version of a tale. These changes are not at all arbitrary. In them reside fundamentals of Judaism and its understanding of the relationship between God and His universe, as well as between one human being and another. Therein, I believe, lies the author's signal contribution.

Morris B. Margolies, PhD

Acknowledgments

With deep gratitude, I acknowledge the generosity of Dov Noy and Edna Hechal at the Israel Folklore Archives in Haifa and Jerusalem. Dov Noy, founder of the archive, is recognized internationally for his knowledge of and dedication to Jewish folklore. I am indebted to him for his time and interest, so graciously given. The assistance of Edna Hechal proved invaluable to the completion of this collection. I also want to thank Aviva Arad, my translator in Israel, for her able assistance.

I am grateful to Rabbi Morris Margolies for his interest in this project. Dr. Carla Klausner's careful reading and feedback are most appreciated. My thanks go to Terry Forge for her secretarial help.

The Enduring Power of Folktales

Since antiquity folktales have captured our hearts with tales of the benevolent and the boorish, the courageous and the corrupt. What attracts us to a genre typically set in far-off lands and distant times with characters portrayed in the simplest of terms? Where did these tales originate? What makes them universal? For whatever reasons, the appeal of folktales persists. They reflect deeply felt cultural beliefs shaped and reshaped to fit local contexts. Something within us welcomes the richness of the folktale, a genre that for all its simplicity is filled with human significance.

Remarkably similar tales appear in vastly differing cultures throughout the world.[1] They maintain common story lines even as each retelling adapts to a particular culture. Over 700 cultural variants of the Cinderella tale, for example, have been documented with at least one Ashkenazic version and one from the Sephardim.[2] Every telling puts its cultural stamp on stories based on the same motifs. There are numerous explanations for finding similar tales in locations separated by land and sea. Some recognize Europe as the source of all tales, explaining that European explorers carried their tales to far-off shores.

Others feel that folktales express a shared, deeply human instinct.[3]

We are indebted to the oral tradition for the preservation of folktales. The informality and immediacy of the spoken word forms indelible connections. Once shared, the tales generally remain a part of both listener and teller. The power of story sustains us with reminders of basic truths and informs a network of threads that binds generations of one cultural group together.

Jewish Folktales

Narrative holds an honored place in the Jewish tradition. Stories have played a crucial role in preserving the Jewish faith by serving as a major learning tool. Since ancient times, the Jewish people have cherished a tradition of learning. Before the availability of written texts, oral stories served as the vehicle for teaching. In addition to the system of teaching behavior, history, and religion emanating from the synagogue, a secular strain of tales flowed from the home, the street, and the marketplace. In time, written texts would come to dominate, but never replace, the telling of tales. From the biblical allegories (*mashal*), to the legends of the Talmud, to the Midrash, which included a written record of oral narrations (*aggadah*), to the Hasidic tales of the Baal Shem Tov, and continuing to this day, Jews have maintained a continuous flow of both oral and written narrative.

While granting that forms of oral and written discourse differ greatly, together they complement each other in providing strong reinforcement for ideas (Ong, 1991).[4] This combination of both written and oral transmission sustained a faith and a culture fraught with extreme challenges to its survival— a remarkable accomplishment for a people repeatedly forced to disperse.

But how does one distinguish Jewish folktales from other folktales? The exchange of story motifs with non-Jews became a common occurrence as a result of living for generations in close proximity to other cultures. What, then, really makes a folktale "Jewish"? Dov Noy describes Jewish tales as containing at least one of the following: a Jewish life cycle (e.g., weddings); a Jewish setting (e.g., synagogue); a Jewish character (e.g., rabbi), or a Jewish message (e.g., hospitality).[5] These characteristics, combined with the source of the tale, help to identify the folktale as "Jewish."

Folk Literature of the Sephardic Jews

A distinctive folk literature developed over the centuries in the Iberian Peninsula and during the interval of the dispersal of the Sephardim that followed. Faced with two choices—death or conversion to Christianity—Jews converted, fled, or became martyrs to their faith. Of those who converted, many continued to practice Judaism in secret. Those who fled went in many directions, taking their faith and a unique Hispanic perspective with them. While maintaining their medieval Hispanic heritage in varying degrees, various traits of Mediterranean, Near Eastern, and European cultures influenced their lives and created a richly distinctive culture in its own right.

Many Sephardim settled in the Ottoman Empire, in North Africa, France, the Balkans, Greece, and the Middle East. In time, they influenced and were influenced by the secular cultures of Christians and Muslims. Tales of the Sephardim often incorporate motifs borrowed from non-Jews. In turn, Christian and Muslim tales borrowed motifs from the Sephardim.

Generations spent living among people of diverse cultures impacted Jewish secular life to the extent that it changed the way Jews spoke. The Iberian Jews developed Judeo-Spanish (Ladino), a language written in Hebrew until the 20th when it began to appear in Latin letters.

Some Jews managed to maintain a Castilian Spanish and retained some ancient Spanish vocabulary, while others abandoned these roots and adopted a mixture of Hebrew with strong Arabic, Greek, and African influences. For example, the Jews in Morocco established a dialect called Haketia tied to Arabic and French. Sounds of African languages appeared among Jews in other parts of North Africa. Dialects grew from exposure to Greek and Turkish in the Balkans, from Arabic throughout the Middle East.

Scholars collected and nourished a body of secular folk literature from Eastern European Jews (the Ashkenazim), some working independently and

some through the Yiddish Scientific Institution (Yivo) in Vilna, Poland, and
New York. No such movement was at work to preserve tales of the Sephardim.
It wasn't until after the establishment of the State of Israel that secular tales of
the Sephardim became well-known.[6]

Contemporary Israel has nourished a cultural resurgence of the Sephardim.
Groups, such as the National Authority for Ladino and its Culture and The
Foundation for Advancement of Sephardic Studies and Culture, work to
assure the survival of its history and language.[7] The contribution of dedicated
individuals cannot be overstated. Among them is Dov Noy, founder and
director of the Israel Folktale Archives (IFA) where tales narrated by the
Sephardim (as well as other immigrants to Israel) have been collected and
preserved since 1955. Another is Matilda Koén-Sarano, who has worked to
perpetuate the culture through her teaching, writing, a Ladino-language radio
show, and informal monthly gatherings where tales are shared.[8] And so the
folk literature of the Sephardim, which evolved into a luscious stew brewed of
varied cultural components while maintaining the taste of its Jewish identity,
continues to grow and enrich our heritage.

Stories in This Collection

The process of selecting tales for this collection was fraught with questions,
not the least of which was how to represent the wit and wisdom found in
tales growing out of a shared origin tempered by generations of life in vastly
differing cultures.

The work of contemporary researchers has preserved a wealth of tales
gleaned directly from Sephardic narrators. The collective memory of these
narrators represents a living treasure of their heritage. However, the process
of transcribing oral renditions into print often diminishes their vitality. As a
result, on the page many tales become brief snippets of their former selves. In
most cases, I combined several stories, retelling them as one tale. In so doing,
I made every effort to conserve a continuity of character and oicotype (a local
tale of a specific region).[9] For example, "The Contrarian" grew out of four

tales. One, from the IFA, contains the idea that "ups in life are followed by downs, and downs by ups." This tale also has ties to the Talmud where Rabbi Akiva illustrates the temporary notion of good and bad luck by smiling at the devastation of Mount Zion and the foxes playing in the ruins of the Temple. The IFA also lists a number of ascension tales—tales of a calling to return to Jerusalem. Another, from *The Oriental Tales of Wisdom*, describes someone who can't make up his mind—he blows on his hands to cool them and blows on his hands to warm them. Still another comes from one of Y. A. Yoná's *Judeo-Spanish Ballad Chapbooks* where the lyrics are reversed to "May Song," a traditional ballad that welcomes springtime.[10]

It is my hope that this collection preserves the tales' original integrity as it reaches out to a broad audience.

The Power of Song

People throughout the kingdom rejoiced when they heard that a boy child, the prince, was born! The boy grew to be strong, handsome, and sweet-tempered. Because everyone loved him, he was the center of joy throughout the land. Each time the king looked at his son, he thought, *Truly, I am blessed.*

But, by the prince's seventh birthday, everyone sensed that something was not right. Rumors could be heard here and there. *The prince cannot learn the Alef Bet!*

The king's sages could not explain why the prince was not learning the alphabet, but each had a plan. The first sage said, "He doesn't learn because he is distracted. Move him to a room with no windows, no pictures on the walls. Then, I guarantee you, oh, king, he will learn the Alef Bet."

Such a room was prepared for the prince. Not a window, a picture, a flower, a toy—nothing was in this room, only two pillows. One was for the prince and the other for the first sage to sit upon.

After many weeks the king called the first sage before him. "So?" asked the king. "How is my son progressing? With no distractions, he must be ready to read Torah. Bring him to me and let me hear him read."

What could the first sage say? After all this time, the boy did not even know the Alef Bet. How could he read Torah?

"Your royal highness," began the first sage, "the prince is strong. He is handsome. He is sweet-tempered. Perhaps that is enough for a prince? With all due respect, honored one, I fear your son cannot learn."

"You ignoramus!" shouted the king. "A prince must be prepared to be king. I know my son can learn! Away with you!" And he banished the first sage from the kingdom.

The king's second sage came forward. "Your royal highness, sir," he said, "the young prince does not learn because he is lonely for other children to learn with. Let me bring children to the palace. We will make a school for the young prince."

That makes sense, thought the king. *He has no playmates. Playmates will inspire him to learn.*

And so the empty room was transformed into a colorful classroom with toys, flowers, and windows that looked out on the garden. There were many laughing children to learn and play with the prince.

The other children learned their letters fast enough, but not the prince. After a time, the king called his second sage before him.

"Tell me," said the king, "how well is my son learning, now that he has other children learning with him? Surely by now he is reading Torah?"

The second sage bowed his head. What could he say? The prince still did not know his letters. So the king banished the second sage from the kingdom.

∽

"Where is my third sage?" demanded the king. "Bring him to me at once!"

The third sage came before the king nervously. "Your Royal Highness," he began, "what the boy needs is to be outdoors. The beauty of nature will inspire him to learn his letters. He will study in the open air and he will learn. Let me have him for a time and I guarantee that he will be reading Torah when you see him next."

"Yes," said the king, "perhaps that is what he needs. Fresh air and sun should do it."

Every morning the boy and the third sage left the castle and returned only after dark. After a time, they both had a healthy glow from their many hours out of doors. But, alas, despite his healthy glow, the prince remained unable to read the Alef Bet.

When the third sage stood before the king, what could he say? "Your son, the prince: he is strong, he is handsome, and he is sweet-tempered, but he has not yet learned his letters. I fear, O honored one, that your son cannot learn."

"What?" shouted the king. "After all this time in the great outdoors, he still cannot read? Away with you!" And the king banished the third sage from the kingdom.

The king felt sadder than he had ever felt before. He began to think the unthinkable—that perhaps his son could never be king. What if his sages were right? Without knowing how to read, it would be easy to trick a king. There were those who would read documents one way when the documents said something else. What was worse, the prince would never know the joy of reading Torah.

The king thought and thought. *I will not believe that my son cannot learn. I know in my heart that he can. He will be a great king. I only have to find the right way to lead him to wisdom. Perhaps he just isn't ready. Perhaps he just needs more time.* So the king decided to wait. What else could he do?

But seeing his son each day without the light of learning was too much for the king to bear. So he sent messengers throughout other lands to seek a teacher who would kindle the light of learning in his son. Many came from far-off lands, but none was able to teach the young prince to read.

Just as his subjects shared the king's joy when the prince was born, so now they shared his sorrow. The land became sad and sullen. Rarely did people smile, and laughter was a thing of the past.

The king began to ride into the countryside away from his court. He would often stop his carriage, get out, and walk. On one of these walks he met an old beggar with a shining face. The beggar asked the king why he was sad.

"Everyone says my son cannot learn. We have tried everything. Nothing works." Then the king thought to himself: *Why am I talking to this beggar? How can he help me?* But, there was something peaceful about this beggar's face that made the king feel that he was speaking to a kindred spirit.

So the king talked to the beggar for a long time. He told the beggar about all his attempts to help the boy learn. "I want to believe that my son can learn, but now I am a bit doubtful myself."

The beggar listened and then said, "You are king. You are powerful. And, you are a righteous man. Your hopes for the boy will be fulfilled—**in song**."

The king laughed at such a silly idea and walked away. After a few days, he forgot all about the old beggar.

News of the prince who could not learn spread far and wide. It reached a young man, a songster, who heard of the boy's plight. *I will go to the land of the prince who cannot learn,* thought the songster. *Perhaps I can be of some help.*

When the songster stood before the king and began to sing, he sang with a voice that sweetened the air and made all who heard it feel at peace. The words were strange. It was a language new to the king.

"What is this song you sing so sweetly? What tongue do you speak?" asked the king.

The young man sang his reply :

> *A songster am I and music's my skill.*
> *A life without song would give me a chill.*
> *I come from a land where singing's the rule.*
> *We sing while we play; we sing while in school.*
> *We sing as we work; we sing as we pray.*
> *The songs fill our life with joy every day.*

The musician sang songs for the king all through the day and into the night. And he explained their meaning in the king's language. This cheered the king beyond memory.

"How can I repay you for this lovely entertainment? Name a gift of your choice."

"It is enough that you found favor in my song, oh, great king. Still, there is someone in this kingdom I want very much to meet."

"Of course. Who could that be?" asked the king.

"I want to meet your son who they say cannot learn. Let me try to help him."

The king's face became sad once more. "No one can help my son. My three brightest sages could not help him. How can you?"

The songster replied with another song in his language. The king asked him to explain its meaning.

"The song asks, 'Can I try? I think I know how to help your son learn.' "

The king could see no harm in it, so he agreed.

When the songster met the boy, he first bowed, looked hard into the boy's eyes, and smiled. When the prince smiled back, the songster tapped his foot three times and sang three simple tones. Inviting the boy to join with him, he tapped his foot and sang three times again. The prince tapped his foot three times as he sang the same tune.

Then the poet began a simple song. Soon the boy joined in. They continued in this manner until they both started to laugh. It was clear that the poet and the boy enjoyed each other. They began to spend their days together— sometimes outside under the sun, sometimes inside with the village children, and sometimes alone. Their meetings were full of song and laughter.

The songster only spoke to the prince in song. Soon they were singing the Alef Bet. They sang the letters into words, sentences, and even jokes.

"Who am I? I am first," sang the songster.

"You are *alef*," sang the prince.

"And who am I? I am last," sang the poet.

The prince sang, "*Tav, tav* is my name."

"Yes," sang the poet, "and while I am last, I am the first letter of the name of the holy Torah."

It wasn't long before the young prince was reading in song. He would sing Torah as he read. Often he sang questions to the poet who sang back answers. Soon he would sing his thoughts about what he read.

∞

The king summoned the songster to him, prepared to hear the worst once more.

"Tell me, musician. Is my son learning? Do not spare me the bad news. I hear he is happily singing, but can he read? Can he read?"

"Sire, your son is strong, he is handsome, he is sweet-tempered."

"Yes, yes. This I know. Answer my question. Can he read?"

"Let me bring forth the prince, oh, most respected king, and he will answer your question," sang the poet.

The prince came to the throne room with the Torah in his hands.

"Let me show you, father," said the prince. Then he began to sing.

To hear the prince read the Torah in song with all the beauty of the words and their meaning filled the king with joy. At last, to know that his son could learn! At last, to know that his son could become a wise king!

"Songster! Musician! Poet! You are a treasure!" exclaimed the king. "You shall have an honored place in my court!"

But the songster was nowhere to be seen. After many attempts to find him, the king realized he must have returned to his land, but where that was no one seemed to know.

As time passed, the king could see that his son was wiser than he by far. *It is time for me to step aside,* thought the king. *I will make my son king now so that during my old age I can take pride in his wisdom.*

And so the prince, now a young man, was made king. All in the land rejoiced, for they knew that he would be a great king. He was strong. He was handsome. He was sweet-tempered. And he was wise beyond his years.

By his side sat the old king, who never once remembered that an old beggar had told him his son would learn "with a song."

About This Tale

What is a king to do when his wise men cannot solve the problem closest to his heart? Just when it seems no one can help, success comes from an unlikely source, a stranger with a shining face who reaches the prince through song.

In Jewish folktales, a "shining face" description usually refers to the prophet Elijah in disguise. Sometimes he is old, sometimes young, sometimes man, sometimes woman, sometimes wise, and sometimes confused. Elijah helps those who are righteous, hospitable, and generous. But those he has helped never know that he intervened on their behalf. Because he represents hope, Elijah has been a favorite character in Jewish stories for generations.

The prophet Elijah has a familiar presence in Jewish life. We set aside a special chair for him at the *brit milah* (circumcision ceremony). We know him as the mysterious guest greeted with an open door and a glass of wine during the Passover seder. And it is Elijah, we are told, who is to announce the coming of the Messiah.

The classic folktale motifs/types that appear in this tale include: rewards and punishments; teachers and pupils; banishment; fate; son succeeding father as king.

The basic idea for "The Power of Song" comes from a story in the third volume of *Legends of the Jews*. According to L. Ginzberg, the collector of these legends, the story has Judeo-Spanish origins and was found in Syria.[11]

What Djoha Needed

Djoha's father worried about his son. Djoha was a good boy—of that he was sure. Still, he knew that Djoha needed something. What that might be, he was not at all sure. *Perhaps,* he thought, *perhaps all Djoha needs is some time—time to find himself.*

Once, Djoha's father asked the boy to take seven donkeys to the market. "Keep a close eye on them, for we will need the price they bring for the long winter."

Djoha did what his father asked. He kept a close eye on the donkeys. Before leaving, he counted them very carefully—one, two, three, four, five, six, seven. Yes, there were seven. To make sure they stayed together, he decided not to lead them in a line, one after the other. He thought: *If I lead the line I can't keep a close eye on the ones in the back, and if I walk behind the line, I can't keep a close eye on the ones in the front.* So, he placed three on either side of the one he mounted. In this way, he could do what his father had ordered: he could keep a close eye on all of them.

After riding along for a while, he thought he would count them again to be sure none were lost. He looked to one side: three donkeys. He looked to the other side: three donkeys. "Wait a minute!" he shouted. "That is only six! What happened to the seventh one?"

He jumped off his donkey and started to count them once more. He touched each one as he counted, "One, two, three, four, five, six, SEVEN! Ah, the missing donkey has come back!" He mounted the middle donkey and continued on his way. This happened two more times before he reached the market. When he finally got there, Djoha noticed that there were three donkeys to one side and three to the other. He jumped off the middle donkey to count them once again. Yes, another miracle! All seven were there.

When he returned home, he handed his father a full purse. "It's a miracle!" Djoha said. "In spite of missing one donkey three times on the way to the market and once again when we arrived., the beast returned each time."

"Really?" his father said, worriedly. "Well, it all worked out well, didn't it? Come now, I'll show you a very secret hiding place for this money pouch. No one must know where we put it, for we need it for the long winter."

A few weeks later, before the first frost, Djoha was home alone when a very tall man, a beggar, came to the door. The man looked hungry. His clothes were faded and torn. "Do you have something for me?" the beggar asked.

"What's your name, sir?"

"Winter—Shlomo Winter."

Djoha gazed up at this very tall man and remembered. "Ah, yes, *Mr. Winter.*" Djoha welcomed him inside and said, "Yes, indeed, we have been expecting you. Please sit and rest a while." Djoha ran to the hiding place, found the pouch of money, and handed it to the beggar. "My father said this would be for a long Winter. Here, go in peace!"

Later, when Djoha explained to his father how happy Mr. Winter had been with the money, his father could only moan. "Djoha, Djoha! You have a kind heart. You did a kind deed, but we still need money for the long winter."

∞

Djoha spent his afternoons at the marketplace visiting with people. One afternoon he saw a lady talking to a man who was looking at a piece of paper.

Djoha noticed that when the lady talked, the man moved something across the paper. He walked over to them and watched. When the lady talked, the man made little dots on the paper. When the lady stood up, she gave the man a shiny gold coin. *What is this?* thought Djoha. *A gold coin for dots on a paper?*

The man told Djoha he wrote letters for people. It was his business. *I can do that!* thought Djoha. *I will write letters and give the gold coins to my father for the long winter.* He ran all the way home to fetch paper and pen. When he returned to the marketplace, he shouted to the people, "Letters! Let me write your letters!" It wasn't very long before an old woman stopped to talk to Djoha.

"Write a letter, young man. Write to my sister, who lives in Salonika, a city far away. Tell her I am no longer sick. Tell her . . . why don't you write what I say?"

"Oh, yes," said Djoha. "Say it again, please."

As she repeated the message, Djoha bent over the paper and moved the pen with each word she said. "*No longer sick.* Yes, I wrote that. What else?" He busily scratched the paper with his pen as she spoke about the *brit milah* of a new grandson, the *bar mitzvah* of her nephew, the wedding she wished her sister could have seen, and much more. When they were finished, she asked for the letter to sign it with her mark.

"What is this?" she shouted. "I know what writing looks like, young man. This is not writing!" She began to scream and pound Djoha about the head. Soon a crowd gathered around them.

"Look!" she shouted to the crowd as she held up the "letter" full of little dots and scribbles. "This boy tricked me. No one can read a letter like this!"

When the crowd saw this, they chased Djoha all the way home.

After Djoha's father sent the crowd away, he said, "My son, we must talk."

"The lady was supposed to give me a shiny gold coin for the long winter!" Djoha wept.

"Yes, a good idea, but first you must learn to write. Don't cry, my son, you just need some time to find yourself. I know now what will help. You need to go to school. Tomorrow, that's where you will go."

"And learn to write?"

"Yes, you will learn to write."

So Djoha started school the next morning.

Each day he ran all the way to school. He ran because he loved school, even though it was hard for him to learn. When the other students laughed at him, he laughed, too, thinking, *What a happy place this is!*

But he also ran because he was late. No matter how hard he tried, he never could get up, get ready, and arrive on time. Each morning when he finally got out of bed, he was alone in the house. His father had stopped trying to wake him and had gone to work. Djoha could never find his clothes. His shirt was on the floor, his shoes under the bed, his pants—where were his pants? He found them in the kitchen. Although he hurried as fast as he could, he arrived at school late.

"Again, you are tardy!" the *hakham*, the rabbi, shouted. "Are you still a baby who needs to sleep all day?" Worse still was the awful teasing Djoha took from the other children. "Baby, baby, sleepy baby!" the children shouted.

One day, the children caught Djoha and took off his shoes. Djoha ran to catch the children, but each time he got close to a boy with his shoes, that boy would toss them to another. Djoha ran back and forth until he was breathless. Finally, he jumped on top of a rock and, showing the meanest face he could muster, shouted in his loudest, most threatening voice, "If you don't give me back my shoes, I . . . I . . . will be forced to do what my father did!" The school yard got suddenly quiet. Slowly, a boy walked up and dropped Djoha's shoes. Then, he ran away. All the other children ran away—all except his one friend, a boy named Moshe.

"Tell me, Djoha, what was it that your father did?" Moshe asked.

"He bought a new pair of shoes," Djoha replied.

∽

Finally, the *hakham* took Djoha aside. "This tardiness must stop," he said. "Here is what you must do. Each night make a list of where you put everything you need for school so that in the morning your list will tell you where everything is. In this way you will come to class on time."

Djoha did as the *hakham* said. That night he made the list of everything he needed in the morning: "The pants are on the chair; the shirt is hanging on a peg on the wall; the socks are under the chair; the shoes are in the kitchen; the schoolbooks are by the door; Djoha is in the bed."

In the morning he looked at his list. He found the pants, the shirt, the socks, the shoes, and the schoolbooks. *This list works fine,* he thought, until he got to the last item on the list. It said, "Djoha is in the bed." He looked in the bed, but Djoha was not there. He looked and looked everywhere for Djoha, but could not find him. Finally, he went to school, and although he ran all the way, he walked into class late once more. Yes, there was more teasing, and this time the *hakham* made him sit in the corner with his face to the wall.

After class, the *hakham* said. "Djoha, did you make a list as I suggested?"

"Yes, yes, *hakham*, sir. And it worked fine until I went to find Djoha. The list said he was in the bed, but he wasn't there. I couldn't find him anywhere, so I came to school late once again."

"Ah, I see," said the *hakham.* "This is not an easy thing, Djoha—to find yourself!" He thought a moment as he scratched his beard. Then he smiled and said, "My boy, here's what you must do: put a mirror on the wall over your bed and tomorrow morning you will find Djoha."

This worked perfectly.

From then on, Djoha never had trouble finding himself.

About This Tale

Like tales of the lovable Ashkenazic fools of Chelm or Libya's fools from Kuzbat, Djoha tales are classified as "numskull" or "fools" tales. For generations the Sephardim have prized Djoha, their simpleton/trickster. He often gets into trouble for following directions literally. This leaves him puzzled, since he always takes special care to do things exactly as he is asked to do them. In spite of being "slow," he often manages to get the upper hand when caught in a challenging situation. We can't help but laugh at his well-intentioned mix-ups and, at the same time, feel a strong fondness for him. Djoha's inherent goodness and innocence make him a favorite among folktale characters.

While tales of Djoha often have him living in Maked (somewhere in Macedonia), we learn of his adventures from Sephardim who have lived in numerous areas.

This story grew out of several Djoha favorites: "Counting the Mules," "The Long Winter," "The Letter Writer," "Late for School," and "Father's Shoes." I found these tales in Haboucha and Koén-Sarano.[12]

Tzohar

It was a time of great sorrow in Jerusalem. Titus, the Roman general, had destroyed the Second Temple in Jerusalem and enslaved the Jews.

Zur was too old to be of much use as a slave, and his grandson Zuriel was too young. When the soldiers took Zuriel's parents away, Zur ran after them. "Why take this young boy's parents?" he shouted. "Take me! Take me!" But the soldiers laughed, "Get out of our way, old man."

Zur and Zuriel walked behind the long line of Jews that the soldiers were taking away. They walked and walked—all the way to the harbor where they watched the soldiers load the captives onto boats. Zuriel kept his eyes on his parents who were waiting in the long line. Once they got on a boat and were out of sight, Zuriel sat down and cried. He had been brave all day, but when he could no longer see his parents, he could be brave no longer. Now, as the boats began to leave the port, his cries rode on the waves and out to sea.

"Where are the boats going?" Zuriel kept asking. He asked the soldiers who were guarding the port and anyone else who would listen, but no one would answer him. Finally, a kindly Roman soldier bent down and whispered into his ear, "Don't cry, little boy. I hear they need workers in Hispania."

On the long walk back to Jerusalem, Zuriel told his grandfather what the soldier had whispered. "Where is Hispania, Grandfather?"

"Far away, my boy, far to the west."

∞

Soon after that, the Roman soldiers forced Zur and his grandson to leave their family home. It had been home to Zur's father, his grandfather, great-grandfather, and great-great-grandfather before him. They were a family of *sofers*, scribes of the holy Torah. Each had taught his son the skill of writing, preparing the parchment, making the ink, and carving the quills. When old age gave Zur an unsteady hand, his son became a *sofer*. Zur had been spending his time caring for the family's library and teaching Zuriel.

Zur's family home had been known as a place to find scrolls, a place to discuss their meanings. Neighbors as well as travelers from far-off lands would stop by to ask for help in translating letters or scrolls written in some foreign language. Some people came with a scroll that needed repair. Others, who fell upon hard times, came to sell a scroll, knowing that here they would receive a fair price. Over time, Zur's family had collected writings on many topics in many languages. People called their home a place of knowledge.

Weeks before the Romans attacked, Zur knew bad times were coming. He saw a sign in the night sky—a star shaped like a sword. Surely this was an omen not to be ignored. He convinced his son to hide their scrolls in a cellar room deep under the house.

∞

Now, the old man and the boy were homeless.

The Roman soldiers ignored them as the two hurried through the streets to find a place to sleep. *I am grateful,* thought Zur, *grateful for how invisible the very old and the very young can be.* The streets were full of soldiers committing unholy acts. Zur and the boy cried quietly as they watched the soldiers burn holy Torahs. Those who wailed their sorrow at the sight were slain, to stop their noise.

It was by accident that they found a place to sleep. Zur was resting against some rocks while Zuriel tossed stones against the wall to the city. The little boy noticed a crack in the wall large enough for him and his grandfather to walk through. Here was a cavelike room inside the great wall of Jerusalem. "Praised be the Lord!" said Zur. "We have found a safe place. If we stay very quiet, how will the soldiers know we are here?" They could hear the Roman soldiers outside shouting and smashing things. They could hear Jews crying for mercy. Zur put his arm around Zuriel and spoke softly. "It is all right, my boy. We are in here; they are out there."

But Zur could not get a picture out of his mind. Each time he closed his eyes he saw a picture of a Torah in flames. He thought of the Torah at his house, the one that his son had nearly completed before the Romans came. He remembered the many scrolls his family had collected for generations—the thoughts of the rabbis, the history of his people—all still there in the cellar room. *Once the soldiers find the scrolls,* thought Zur, *they will surely burn them.*

His greatest wish was to save every scroll of Jewish learning. But that was impossible. The soldiers burned and desecrated all the Torah scrolls in the Temple. "Maybe, Zuriel, just maybe we can save all our scrolls before the soldiers discover them. We can bring them back here for safe keeping."

So, in the days that followed, the old man and the boy would leave their hiding place before first light and walk to their old home. Then, after dark, they would return to safety inside the wall. With each trip they carried as many scrolls as they could without being noticed. It was hard work for an old man and a young boy, but Zur was determined to make as many trips as he could.

One night, heavy with fear and exhaustion, they rested inside the wall. Zuriel finally fell asleep. As the old man closed his eyes, once again he saw the Torah aflame. He sat up and stared into the darkness.

He noticed a glimmer of light resting on the ground with sparks that lit up the night. Fearful that the light would disappear, he moved toward it with soft, catlike steps. *What is this?* he wondered. Bending down, he saw a small stone glowing with a warm, blue light. Zur picked it up, turned the stone over and over in his hand admiringly, and put it in his pocket.

Soon he fell asleep—a deep and dreamy sleep. He dreamed he was swimming through a sea of warm blue light emanating from the stone in his pocket. The stone's light led him back, back, back to before the earth was born. There he watched the stone fall into the never-ending Blackness where it grew and grew, forming the earth itself. How lovely was this earth with its grasses and forests, its mountains and deserts, its lakes and oceans. Then, here was the stone, small once again, as it appeared before Adam and Eve. Wild-eyed with fright, they grasped the stone as they fled the garden. Its sparks revealed a glimpse of the unfamiliar world they were to enter. Next, Zur saw Noah at the window of his ark holding up the iridescent stone to greet the scent of dry land. And then he saw the stone become the altar where Abraham placed Isaac for sacrifice. The altar glowed amid tears of faith and gratitude. And, finally, he recognized the stone as the rock on which the Temple was built.

Zur woke to the sound of heavy footsteps. Roman soldiers surrounded them. "What is this?" one shouted. "An old man and a boy resting on a bed of scrolls? Burn the scrolls and the Jews, too!" They laughed and began kicking the scrolls into a large pile. Remembering what Romans did to those who cried loudly, Zuriel cried as quietly as he could.

"Out!"

Suddenly, the soldiers stood still. Their officer had entered the wall and was ordering them all outside. Once Zur was alone with the Roman officer, he felt sure their time had come.

"Do what you will to me, sir, but have mercy on my grandson and these scrolls!"

"I am Didius, centurion in the army of Titus. We have been watching you and the boy going out before light and in after dark with these scrolls." He pulled several out of the pile and read their titles. "I see here works in Greek, and Latin, but these other tongues I do not recognize. Who are you?"

"I am Zur, *sofer* for the word of the one Lord."

"What is a *sofer*?"

"I, my son, and my family before me, are scribes for the holy word of our Lord."

"Then you know these works? Where do they come from?"

"I know them. They come from my family library in my house."

"Come, we must go there at once. You will teach me these tongues."

"I will not go without my grandson!"

"So be it." The officer called to his men and commanded them to carry all the scrolls carefully, while marching Zur and Zuriel back to their home.

When they arrived, Didius was amazed when he saw the scrolls buried in Zur's house. In Rome only the wealthiest families had scrolls, and rarely as many as he saw here. He decided to move into Zur's home. The old man feared he and Zuriel would be thrown out once more, but to his amazement, this Roman officer wanted him to stay. He wanted to study with Zur.

Imagine, thought Zur, *a Roman who loves learning!* Didius met with Zur and Zuriel each evening to learn Hebrew and Aramaic so he could read his way through the library.

During the day, Zur taught Zuriel the *sofer*'s craft. The boy was beginning to write the Alef Bet with a firm hand, but it would be many years before he could master the spacing, the intricate designs for certain letters—all the many fine details for a *sefer Torah*. "You must practice, boy. Remember absolutely no errors are permitted when writing the Lord's words." He wondered if he would live long enough to complete Zuriel's training.

It troubled Zur to think that possibly no Torah had survived the Roman fires. He found the Torah his son could not finish before the Romans came. When he opened it to the place where the words stopped, he knew what he must do. Then he glanced down at his hands. *I will pray for a steady hand.*

Zuriel helped his grandfather prepare the parchment. He collected feathers for Zur to carve into quill pens. He helped grind gallnuts into a fine powder for the ink. He watched carefully as Zur made all the preparations. When all was ready, Zur went to the *mikveh* to make himself clean. He fasted and prayed to sanctify his heart to be a vessel for the holy words. Then, he sat at the table, ready to begin. But when he picked up the quill, his hand shook so terribly that he put it down quickly. He sat for a long time without moving.

"I know, Grandfather," said Zuriel. "Hold the shining stone. It brought us good luck before. Perhaps it will again."

Zur pulled the stone out of his pocket and cupped it for a few minutes in both his hands. Then he set it on the table next to the ink. This time when he picked up the quill, his hand was as steady as in the days of his youth.

∞

In a few months, the Torah was completed, and Zur rested peacefully for the first time since the Romans conquered Jerusalem.

But his peacefulness was short-lived.

A senior Roman officer, the Primus Pilus, had heard that Didius was living with Jews. It was not unusual to take Jewish property, but to live with Jews? This he found hard to believe. When he went to Zur's house and found it was true, he commanded his men to arrest the centurion.

"Wait!" said Didius. As he talked to the intruder, Zur and Zuriel hid in the cellar.

Zur gave Zuriel the Torah he had just completed and placed the bright shining stone in his grandson's hand. "Keep these safe, my boy. Go now! Run to the harbor and sail to Hispania. May the lord protect you."

"Come with me, Grandfather."

"No, my child. They will want a Jew and they will have one. I am too old to run. You must go now, before they surround the house."

Zuriel did reach Hispania. And although he never returned to the home where his father, his grandfather, his great-grandfather, and his great-great-grandfather before him had been *sofer*s, scribes of the holy Torah, he continued the family tradition in Hispania. He held the shining stone close throughout his life, and when old age gave him an unsteady hand, he passed the stone, along with the skill of the *sofer*, to his son, and he to his son throughout the generations.

About This Tale

Every culture has a "creation tale"—an explanation for how the earth began. There are a number of creation tales in the Jewish tradition. The Tzohar is believed to be a luminous stone that holds the primordial light of creation. After the Fall, an angel gave the Tzohar to Adam, who passed it on to his children. In Genesis it appeared as a small window in Noah's ark that illuminated the future. Another version had Abraham returning to heaven, where he placed it on the sun. Still another says that the righteous of each generation will have access to the Tzohar.[13]

This tale takes place in a time that represents one of the heaviest memories of the Jewish people: the defilement of the Second Temple by Titus in Rome. During the years of Roman occupation preceding this, Jews had been sent as slaves to Hispania, the Iberian Peninsula. When the Temple was destroyed, Jews fled in many directions. One destination, as in our tale, was Hispania, where the Sephardic community was forming.

Two major sources inspired this retelling: the rich resource of Ginzberg's *Legends of the Jews*, and *Sepher ha-Yashar*,[14] one of the latest works of the midrashic *aggadah*. In the latter, there is a reference to an old man, a lone Jew discovered by a Roman soldier of Titus, who was hiding inside a wall with all the scrolls—all the knowledge—in the world.

Blancaniña

Rico Franco, the Moor, went hunting with his falcon. The hunting fared so poorly that Rico Franco, restless and hungry, gave the falcon three hard blows upon the head and shouted, "Go off, you no-good feathers. Go off and this time bring us back a bite to eat!"

Flying high above the countryside, the falcon saw a golden castle. It landed atop a turret, flew into the courtyard, and rested at a young lady's windowsill. She lay sleeping on her cot. What a true beauty: hair black as the night, parted in the middle with a small bow at the brow; her waistcoat colorful and tight fitting; her stockings shear enough to show a well-turned ankle.

The falcon turned its attention to a pond in the courtyard where ducks were floating peacefully. As quick as a breath, the bird swooped down, grasped a duck in its talons, and returned to Rico Franco.

When the young lady awoke, she ran to her father. "Father!" she cried. "I dreamed a falcon flew to my windowsill. It spoke to me."

"Not so fast, Blancaniña! A tale told slowly is better understood."

Blancaniña began again to tell the dream, slowly at first, but faster and faster as it rolled off her tongue. "I spoke with a falcon. 'Soon you will come away with me,' it said. 'The Moor will take care of you as he does of me—

meanly and without mercy. He will come here and win the game. He will make you his bride, but do not go with the Moor. He will take over the castle. He will enslave your family, your father as his cook, your mother as his laundress, your brothers as workers in a foreign land!' "

"Do not fret, Blancaniña," her father said. "You will never marry a Moor. You will marry a Jew as your mother did, and her mother, and her mother, and all the mothers before her. Remember, it was but a dream."

In fact, Blancaniña's father loved his daughter dearly and could not think of parting with her. *When she comes of marrying age,* he thought, *I will let it be known that I will give her to a suitor neither for gold, nor land, nor goods, but for a wager in a game of chess. This will surely keep her with me, since I always win at chess.*

"Father," Blancaniña said, "I fear the dream will prove true."

In two years' time, suitors began to visit the castle. Blancaniña's father posted a notice on the castle gate:

To all who come to woo my daughter,
Bring neither gold, nor land, nor goods.
Bring but your wits to win her hand in a game of chess.

Each young man who played chess with her father lost the game, and lost Blancaniña.

Then, one Monday morning, Rico Franco, the Moor, appeared, offering gold and land for Blancaniña's hand. Her father reminded Rico Franco that the notice specified neither gold nor land.

"Then a game of chess it is," said the Moor. But this time, Blancaniña's father refused. "Only those of our faith are eligible for this marriage," he said.

"Not so!" challenged the Moor. "Your notice gives no mention of faith. *'To all who come to woo my daughter . . .'* These are your words exactly. A binding statement if I ever heard one." With a smile, he added, "Would you go against your own words, sir?"

"You shall have your game, then, but not today . . . tomorrow."

"No, sir. I insist we play today!"

"You tax my patience, Moor!" But after thinking a long time, Blancaniña's father said, "All right. We play tonight. First be my guest for dinner and then we play."

Once the Moor left, Blancaniña began to tremble. She begged her father not to play with the Moor. "Remember my dream, Father. It foretold the ruin of our family."

"You worry needlessly, Daughter. Am I not always the winner at chess?"

Blancaniña was not pacified. It was Monday, after all, a bad day for taking chances.

∽

Rico Franco sat down to sup with Blancaniña's family. Platters of food rested on salt. Underfoot, boots scraped against salt. There was salt under all but the Moor's chair. Blancaniña herself placed it around the room to protect her family. She made sure there was a knife to guard against evil for everyone at the table—everyone but Rico Franco. When he went to cut his meat, the Moor noticed this. "Ah, no matter," he said, and reached for the dagger at his side.

When the game was about to begin, Blancaniña led Rico Franco to the red cushioned chair at the chess table. This was the one seat cushion she had not salted. "No, no," said the Moor with a smile. "I prefer the black cushion—black as my fair lady's hair."

The room went quiet as a mountaintop when the game began. Rico Franco played at an unusually slow pace. A smile never left his face as he studied the chessboard. When finally he made a move, it was with a great flourish as if in a dance. The minute his hand released a chessman, Blancaniña's father moved his chessman and waited for the Moor once again. All eyes stared intently at the chessboard as the game dragged on. Blancaniña twisted her hair nervously, awaiting her fate.

Suddenly, in a whir of feathers, the Moor's falcon flew through the window and around the room. Everyone glanced up in surprise. When they did, Rico

Franco, now moving very fast, rearranged the chessmen to his advantage.

"Checkmate!" shouted the Moor, pulling Blancaniña into his arms. "The beautiful maiden is mine!" Then, in a voice full of anger, "Blast you, falcon! What took you so long? You'll be punished for this."

Blancaniña's father protested. "Unfair! Unfair! You changed the board to your advantage, sir. I must protest!"

"You must protest!" repeated Rico Franco in a voice full of mockery. "You can protest all you want: this maid is now mine."

As the Moor held Blancaniña close, she reached inside his cloak, drew out his dagger, and raised it to strike him in the heart. But the falcon had its own plans. The bird grasped the dagger from Blancaniña's hand and tossed it across the room.

"Good work, my fine feathers," Rico Franco said, but the falcon began to fly round and round the Moor making angry screeching sounds. Finally, it landed on Rico Franco's shoulder and began pecking out his hair. Its sharp talons dug deep scratches on the Moor's head and face.

"Away! Away, you beast!" shouted the Moor. But the falcon would not stop. Finally, the Moor ran out of the dining hall and through the castle gate with the falcon still at his head. No one ever saw Rico Franco again.

The falcon returned to become Blancaniña's pet and protector. Wherever she went, the falcon was with her resting gently on her shoulder.

After Blancaniña's father tore the notice from the castle gate, many young men came to ask for her hand. As her father predicted, she married a Jew just as her mother did, and her mother, and her mother, and all the mothers before her. And the one she picked was wise beyond his years. Rather than take Blancaniña to a new home far from her family, which she held so dear, he built a castle for her right next to her father's. And there (along with the pet falcon) they lived out their days happily and in peace.

About This Tale

Blancaniña is a version of a 16th century ballad known as *Rico Franco*. It has appeared in different forms and locations throughout the Sephardic communities of Europe and the Middle East. This version incorporates several folktale types/motifs commonly found in the genre: the notion that Mondays are bad luck days, that salt will protect from evil, that a knife placed on a table or under a bed will keep harm away, and that a bird reveals impending harm.

This tale comes from the Sephardim of Rhodes, Greece. It was derived from one of the many ballads collected by Y. A. Yoná who gathered traditional ballads from the Sephardic communities of Salonika, Greece, and Sofia, Bulgaria, in the late 19th and early 20th centuries. Published in Ladino (Judeo-Spanish Hebrew), the ballards appeared in eight chapbooks. His work makes up the first volume of Armistead and Silverman's collection of literature of the Sephardim.[15]

A Friend for a King

Long ago and far away, there lived a king. He had great wealth—fine jewels, beautiful gardens, and several castles. He had a crown to wear during the week, a crown that was a little fancier to wear on the weekends, and a very fancy crown to wear on special occasions. He treated his subjects fairly and with kindness. They returned his kindness with respect and awe. Still, the king was not happy.

He was tired of watching everyone bow down and address him so carefully. "Oh, Great Sire, Your Glorious Highness, Honored Sir," they said.

Why can't people talk to me as they would to an ordinary man? the king wondered. He yearned for a friend. *Oh, for a true and simple friendship! What could be more precious?* It was the only thing he did not have.

One day, he decided to do something about it. He would shed the crown and his royal robes and walk through his kingdom as a common man. In this way, he thought, *people will feel free to befriend me because they will not see a king, but an ordinary man. They will talk to **me**!*"

When the vizier, the wisest of all the king's advisers, heard this, he wasted no time in expressing his concern. "I strongly recommend against it."

"And why is that, Vizier?"

"You will be at risk, Honored Sire. You could come to some harm, because even a poor man will surely recognize your kingly qualities. Do not do this, I beg you!"

"You worry needlessly, Vizier. I am king, after all, so I will do as I wish."

"Then at least let me accompany you, Sire," begged the vizier, "to be sure you come to no harm."

"There will be none of that!" said the king in his most kingly voice. "Have you no faith in my people? I will come to no harm. If they see me as an ordinary man, they could see me as a friend. A *friend*, Vizier—a true friend is more precious than jewels or gold. A friend is the one thing I need."

The king walked out of the castle dressed as an ordinary man with no kingly robes and no crown. But he wasn't alone. Unbeknownst to the king, the vizier followed him at a distance.

As the king strolled through his kingdom, he looked at everyone and everything. He enjoyed what he saw. He loved being among his people. The king smiled at them, but each time he tried to talk to someone, he was pushed aside with, "Go away, old man. I have no time to talk to a stranger."

The king noticed one man who was not hurrying. He looked poorer than the others, and although his clothes were worn thin and his sandals needed mending, he walked with his head high and with a sure step. The king decided to follow him. *Perhaps he will not be too busy to talk to me,* thought the king.

When the poor man stopped in front of his home, the king asked, "May I speak with you, sir?"

"Of course," said the poor man. "Come in. We will have coffee and talk as long as you wish." The poor man introduced himself, his wife, and three sons. "I am Sar Shalom. This is my wife, Asilah, and these are my sons, Ovadia, Salman, and Sancho. And who are you?"

The king did not know what to say. He could not say he was the king. That would ruin his plan. Yet, he could not make up a name and deceive this kind man. He just said, "My name? It doesn't matter, does it?"

His host smiled. "Of course not."

It pleased the king to find that one of his subjects offered the hospitality of his home without knowing his guest's name. It was a poor home, indeed. The dirt floor, which had been carefully swept, had only one ragged rug and five thin cushions. A faded curtain covered the one window. Glancing around, the king noticed a fancy key hanging on the wall. It seemed too fine for such a modest home.

The king and his host sat on two of the cushions on the rug and drank coffee. They talked about everyday things. After they had talked a long time, the king asked about the fancy key hanging on the wall.

"It is the *soudades,* the key to my ancestors' home in a land to the west and north across the sea. We have kept it to remind us that we had to leave our homeland."

"Do you want to return there?" asked the king.

"It would not be wise now. I fear too much time has passed. We would not be welcome; our house would be gone. Still, my father gave me the key that was given to him by his father and I will give it to my sons. In this way we remember what we cannot forget."

Because the poor man looked sad as he thought about this, the king changed the subject. "Tell me," he asked, "do you like riddles?"

"Indeed I do," said the poor man. "But, I must warn you. I am very good at solving them."

"All the better!" laughed the king. He began to tell a riddle that no one in his court had been able to solve: "Once a mosquito and the wind argued. The wind thought it was a silly argument, but not the mosquito. The mosquito lived in the country near the stream where he had hatched. It was far from town. Because no people lived nearby, the mosquito had no one to sting. This meant that he could not get a tasty meal. Every time the mosquito tried to fly into town, he had to turn back. The mosquito was angry. *A mosquito needs to live!* he thought. He decided to consult King Solomon, famous for his wise decisions. But he was never able to do so. Here is the riddle: Why is it that the mosquito could not bring the wind to trial in King Solomon's court?"

The poor man quickly replied, "Because every time the mosquito tried to come to court, the wind blew him away."

The king was surprised by the poor man's quickness. Each time he had posed riddles to his courtiers, they were unable to solve them. Now he realized this was probably because they were afraid to appear smarter than the king. Here was a simple man who answered his king honestly.

"Here's a riddle for *you*," said the poor man. "Who do you think is the strongest: the wind, the cold, or the heat?"

The king thought for a long time. "The wind is the strongest," he finally said.

"Why do you say that?" asked the poor man.

"Because in winter when the wind blows, it makes the cold colder and in summer when the wind blows, it makes the heat cooler."

"Yes!" said the poor man.

The king then asked, "Who can speak in every language?"

The poor man answered quickly. "It is Echo! Here's another one for you. What do you have that everyone else uses more than you?"

The king smiled and replied, "My name."

They continued in this way, exchanging riddles and enjoying each other's company.

"Everybody loves me, yet no one can look at me. What am I?" asked the king.

The poor man replied, "The sun!" Then he asked, "It's not a shirt, yet it's sewed. It's not a tree, yet it's full of leaves. It's not alive, yet it talks wisely. What is it?"

"A book!"

"Very good!" said the poor man. "I'm glad to meet a new friend who is so wise. You are wise enough to be a king!"

At this, the king laughed heartily. But what had the poor man said? "Glad to meet a **new friend**?" This made the king feel so good that he decided to tell his host his real identity.

"Ah, ha!" said the king. "And you are wise enough to recognize your king!"

At first the poor man was so awed to know that the king was in his home that he could think of nothing to say or do. Then he stood up stiffly.

"Oh, no! No!" said the king. "You are my friend. No need to stand. Come, sit with me once more."

Sitting again, the poor man said, "If a king can see a poor man like me as a friend, truly he is a king to be honored."

"Enough of this, good friend," insisted the king. "Because I have enjoyed this visit so much, I want to reward you. I will grant you three wishes. What shall they be?"

The poor man thought hard. Remembering that the king liked riddles, he decided to give his three wishes in the form of a riddle. "My three sons need their education. Perhaps you could help?"

"But, of course! What professions do they want to learn?" asked the king.

"You will know once you solve a riddle."

This pleased the king so much that he laughed again and insisted his friend tell the riddle.

The poor man explained. "All my sons seek professions on the very highest levels. For this riddle, however, see if you can name their professions when I describe them to you at their very lowest levels."

The king smiled his approval, enjoying every minute.

"Son number one, Ovadiah, wants the kind of work that will never pay him enough. He wants to be an honored beggar. Son number two, Salman, wants work that will require him to take things away from people. You could say he wants to be a respected thief. And son number three, Sancho, wants work that often makes him face death. He wants to be a beloved murderer. Tell me what professions they want."

This puzzled the king. He thought hard for a long time. He got up and walked around. "All of these professions are at a very high level, you say?" He wondered how a beggar, a thief, and a murderer could be considered high-level professions.

First, he scratched his head. He scratched his beard. Then, he scratched the end of his nose. At last, he had to say that he could not solve this riddle. This was hard for the king to say because he had never given up on a riddle before. And yet, he was not angry. It delighted him to know such a hard riddle.

"What a prize of a riddle, my friend!" said the king. "I must know the answer."

"The son who wants to be an honored beggar will be a rabbi. The son who wants to be a respected thief will be a lawyer. And the son who wants to be a beloved murderer will be a doctor."

The king stood up and laughed so loud that the poor man's wife and sons came running into the house to see what had happened.

"Come to my castle in three days and your wishes will be granted!" said the king. "But only," he added, "on one condition—that you do not tell it to another until you see my face again. This is such a good riddle that I want to use it as a test for the wisest of the wise men in my court."

The poor man agreed.

Back at his castle the next day, the king summoned the vizier, the wisest of his wise men. "We shall see who is wise and who is not," the king said. "If you are smart enough to solve this riddle, you can remain my main vizier. If you cannot, I will banish you from the kingdom."

The vizier listened to the riddle. "Give me time, O Gracious King!" he begged. "I will consult my assistants. This is a true puzzle of a riddle. I need time to think it through."

"If one of my subjects, a poor, simple man, was able to invent this riddle, surely the wisest man in my kingdom should be able to solve it. You have until tomorrow."

"Thank you, O Wise and Generous King," said the wise man, bowing.

∞

Now, remember, the vizier had followed close behind as the king went strolling in the town. He had seen the house where the king spent the afternoon. He had heard the king's laughter and had seen the king's happy face as he left the house. As fast as he could, he returned to the poor man's house with all his assistants, determined to find the answer to the riddle.

Imagine the poor man's surprise when he opened the door to his house. Standing there were the king's vizier and all his assistants!

"Come in. Welcome to my humble home. What can a poor, simple man like myself do for you great men?"

When the poor man heard the vizier's request, he refused, remembering his promise to the king to tell no one until he saw the king's face once more.

"You must tell me! The king needs the answer!" shouted the vizier. "It is of the utmost importance!"

"But the king knows the answer. Why does he need to know it once more?"

The vizier took a pouch filled with one thousand gold coins from his robe and spilled them out before the poor man. "The king has lost his memory. He sent me to ask you," lied the vizier.

This seemed strange, thought the poor man. *The king showed no problem with his memory yesterday.* He looked carefully at the gold coins. Then he realized what he must do. He told the vizier and his assistants the solution to the riddle and put the gold coins in a safe place.

∞

On the third day the poor man went to the king's court as promised. He found a very sad king slouched down on his throne. "I am the poor man now, sir!" shouted the king. "Three days ago I had a friend. Today, I have none. How could you break your promise not to tell the riddle's answer until you saw my face once more? You were my first and only friend. This is my saddest day!"

"But Sire," laughed the poor man. "You have no need for sadness. I kept my promise, truly!"

"How can that be? My vizier confessed where and how he found the answer. You took one thousand gold coins for the answer! I thought you were a true friend," said the king.

"And that I am, my king. You said not to tell the answer to the riddle until I saw your face again. I saw your face one thousand times on each of the gold coins!"

The king sat up and laughed. "Of course!" He laughed louder and louder until he nearly slid off his throne. "Of course, dear friend, you are surely the wisest of all my advisers. I hereby declare you my new vizier to stand by my side at all times!"

The old vizier was banished to a land far away. Each of the poor man's sons received his education. And the new vizier and the king lived long and fruitful lives full of the joy of a beautiful friendship.

About This Tale

This tale reminds us to prize friendship. A king yearns for a true friend—something that all his wealth and power cannot buy. A poor Jew becomes a friend to the king through honesty, hospitality, and an exchange of riddles. The riddle motif appears frequently in Jewish folktales. The ability to solve riddles reassured Jews, whose low status and lack of wealth or power was beyond their control. While they had little else, they could take pride in knowing they were good thinkers—often good enough to out-smart those who had control over them.

Our tale mentions a key that hangs on the wall of the poor Jew's home. There is a tradition among some Sephardim to display a key—supposedly the key to the home their ancestors were forced to leave during the Inquisition. The key, handed down from generation to generation, reminds them of their Spanish roots.

"A Friend for a King" grew from parts of several tales told by Jewish immigrants to Israel from lands once known as Persia and Babylon. These tales were found in the Israel Folklore Archives at the University of Haifa.

Zipporah and the Seven Walnuts

Once there was a beautiful girl named Zipporah. Her hair, her eyes, and her skin were as dark and sparkling as the nighttime sky. She lived in a far-off land ruled by a kindly sultan. Zipporah lived in the *mellah yahudi*, a separate section of the town where all Jewish families lived. They spoke differently, wore different clothes, ate different foods, and sang different music from everyone else in the kingdom, but they all lived together peacefully.

Zipporah's father was a merchant whose work took him to distant lands. He traveled to sell leather, copper, and silver things made by the craftsmen and women in the *mellah yahudi*. He returned with rare silks, jewels, and spices. Most of these treasures went to the sultan. Zipporah's father sold all the rest, except for one trunk that he packed full of surprises for his family.

Now, next door to Zipporah and her family lived a *brusha*, a very bad witch. This *brusha* could turn her seven daughters into snakes and back into daughters. When Zipporah's father came home from trips, the *brusha* would peek through a window to watch as Zipporah took beautiful things out of the trunk. Oh, how that witch wanted those pretty things for herself!

She had a plan. *I will give them a gift of magic honey. One taste, and Zipporah's father will be under my spell. Then he will marry me and all those pretty things will be mine. My snaky girls will see to the mother.* She prepared the magic honey, turned her daughters into snakes, and put them into a fancy honey pot.

When Zipporah opened the door, the witch smiled her sweetest smile and spoke in her sweetest voice. "Dear girl, please ask your parents to accept this poor gift to welcome your father home." Zipporah's parents accepted the neighborly gift with thanks. As her mother opened the pot, her father put his little finger into the honey jar and tasted the honey. The spell worked. At once a snake bit Zipporah's mother and she died.

After her father married the *brusha*, Zipporah's life changed. The stepmother and her seven daughters spoke unkindly to Zipporah. They kept her working every waking minute. They made fun of her hair, her eyes, and her skin, as dark as the nighttime sky. "Hard work is not as hard to bear as those unkind words," Zipporah cried to her father.

"Yes, my dear, but what can I do?" asked her father. "Come, let's play Walnuts."

Zipporah loved to play Walnuts with her father. They would take seven walnuts and crack them carefully so each player would have seven half shells. After they placed threads on the rug to make squares, they would take turns moving the shells until the winner reached the other side. When the stepmother saw how happy they were, she made the walnuts fly off the rug and disappear. "Back to work, Zipporah!" she shouted.

∞

Now, when Zipporah's father went on trips, the stepmother and her seven daughters waited eagerly for his return, not because they missed him, but because they wanted that trunk full of gifts. When he returned, the seven daughters and their mother ran to the trunk and started pulling out all the pretty things.

"I want that blue silk," said one daughter.

"No, I saw it first," said another.

"That's enough!" said their mother. "The blue silk is mine!"

After they left the room, Zipporah's father shook his head and said, "Looks like they have taken everything. I am sorry, Zipporah, dear, but what can I do?"

Just then, Zipporah thought she heard something move in the bottom of the trunk. She was disappointed to find nothing but seven walnuts rolling about. She put them in her pocket and finished scrubbing the kitchen floor.

∞

Then one day, the whole town learned that the sultan had invited everyone to a fancy ball. It was no secret that the prince, the sultan's son, was looking for a bride. Every girl dreamed of being the prince's bride.

The stepmother helped her daughters make party dresses with the beautiful silks Zipporah's father had brought from distant lands. As she watched them fix each other's hair, the stepmother thought, *With all this finery, surely the prince will not notice their many faults and want to marry one of them. Then I can live where I should—in a palace!*

Zipporah, of course, was not getting ready for the ball. She was hard at work. "Zipporah!" shouted her stepmother. "Come here at once!" She pointed to a pot on the stove. "This pot has oil, flour, and sugar all mixed together." She smiled a sly smile. "After you have separated them, you, too, can come to the ball."

The seven daughters, dressed in their fine gowns, laughed and danced around Zipporah. "You can forget about going to the ball," said one. "You will never separate oil, flour, and sugar. And, even if you did," said another, "you have nothing but rags to wear." They messed up her hair and pulled the skirt of her faded dress.

When they all had gone to the ball, Zipporah looked at the oil, flour, and sugar and wondered, *How could anyone ever separate this stuff? It's impossible!* One tear fell down her dark-as-night cheek. She thought, *I will never go to the ball. I'll never meet the prince.*

Zipporah reached into her pocket and pulled out the seven walnuts. Perhaps eating one walnut would cheer her up. But, which one? When she lined them up, one rolled toward her, as if to say, "Look at me! Open me first!" Zipporah laughed and cracked it open.

WHOOSH! Smoke and wind came out of the walnut. Then, a *djinn* appeared! A giant of a man, black like Zipporah, stood looking down at her. "Separate oil, flour, and sugar? No problem!" As soon as he said this, the task was done. But, the pleasure of seeing such a trick didn't last.

"Now, why are you so sad?" asked the *djinn*. After Zipporah explained what the witch had done to her family, the *djinn* said, "This will never do! I can take care of *brushas*! Bring me some salt." When she brought him the salt, he pushed her away. "No, No! If I touch it, I'll disappear. It is powerful stuff! You take it and sprinkle some under the *brusha's* favorite cushion. She will lose all her powers over anyone who sits on that pillow."

"Oh, now I can go to the ball!" said Zipporah. "But, look at me. I cannot go wearing these rags."

"Not to worry, Little One," said the giant *djinn*. "Look inside the other walnuts."

As Zipporah opened each walnut, she was amazed at what she found: a beautiful dress, boots made of the softest red leather, a lacy fan with rainbow-colored ribbons, a tiara made of seven diamond-studded walnuts, a coachman with a team of white horses, and a gilded carriage with a walnut crest on its door.

"Now!" said the *djinn* in a booming voice. "It is time for the ball. But, Little One, remember this: You must leave at the proper time."

"How will I know the proper time?" asked Zipporah.

"I will be waiting nearby. Listen for me to say 'now' like this: **Now!**" His voice roared like thunder.

When Zipporah arrived at the castle, her dark beauty caused people to stop and stare. They were puzzled because they did not know who she was. "She must be a princess from a far-off land," they said. "Yes, look! Those are real diamonds in her tiara."

The stepmother and seven daughters had no idea that it was Zipporah. But they knew that they did not like this dark, beautiful stranger. "It's not fair!" pouted one sister. "The prince dances every dance with her." "What's worse," said the stepmother, "is that they only have eyes for each other."

The *djinn* waited nearby, but soon fell asleep. When he awoke and remembered Zipporah, he jumped up and shouted, "**Now!**" in his booming voice. "Zipporah, **now!**"

But Zipporah heard only the music and saw only the prince's eyes looking into her own.

"**Now!** Zipporah, **now!**"

Zipporah stopped dancing. She suddenly remembered what she was to do. "Run, Zipporah!" shouted the *djinn*.

Zipporah started to run. She ran so fast that one of her red leather boots fell off. Outside, the carriage was gone. The giant *djinn* was gone. Her beautiful gown was gone. Now wearing her ragged old dress, Zipporah saw nothing on the road but a few walnut shells. She smiled sadly as she picked them up, put them in her pocket, and slowly walked home.

∞

Zipporah's hard life went on as before. She saved the walnut shells and strung them into a necklace that she wore everyday. They reminded her of her one happy night at the ball.

Meanwhile, the prince was sick with love for the princess who had disappeared. Determined to find her, he traveled to far-off lands to seek the one whose foot fit the soft red leather boot she left behind. Finding no one, he returned home, took to his bed, and refused to eat.

"Someday you will be sultan with a beautiful sultana by your side," said his father. "There are other princesses. Now, you must eat something. Here, I will crack a walnut for you."

As the prince took a bite of the walnut, he remembered the walnuts in the lost Princess's tiara. He sat up and said, "I have not looked everywhere. I have not yet looked right here in our own land!" The prince knocked on every door seeking his true love. But, alas, not one girl's foot could fit the red leather boot.

I've lost her, he thought.

On his way back to the castle, he saw houses where the road turned. "Have we tried these homes?" he asked.

"Not there," said his aide. "This is the *mellah yahudi* sector. You will not find your princess in this part of town."

"I will see if that is so," said the prince.

When the witch heard the prince was coming to every house in the neighborhood, she called her daughters together. "Now, girls," she told them, "when it is your turn to try the prince's boot, sit here." She puffed up her favorite cushion (the one with the salt underneath). Each of the stepmother's seven daughters tried, but no one could fit into the red leather boot. The prince was about to leave when Zipporah's father called, "Wait! There is another young lady in this house. Come out of the kitchen, my daughter."

When Zipporah entered the room, the prince noticed her walnut necklace and knew at once he had found his true love. "Please," said the prince, "sit here and put your foot in this boot."

When Zipporah sat on the cushion, the *brusha* tried spell after spell to send her back to the kitchen, but of course, none worked (remember the salt under the cushion!). Zipporah's foot fit the boot perfectly.

The prince asked Zipporah's father for her hand in marriage. "Please give us your blessing. She is my own true love."

Zipporah's father looked at his daughter—so young, so good, so kind. He looked at the prince—so young, so strong, so fine. Both faces glowed with happiness. He looked away for a very long time. When he looked back, he said, "Surely this was meant to be."

They then went to the castle to meet with the sultan. As they approached the throne, the sultan asked, "Who are these people with my son? Who is that man?" His aide whispered in his ear, "He is the merchant who brings you fine things from far-off lands."

Ah, yes. He has served me well, remembered the sultan.

The prince said, "This is Zipporah, my own true love, and this is her father. We wish to be married. We have come for your blessing."

The sultan looked at his son—so young, so strong, so good. He looked at Zipporah—so young, so fair, so dark. Both faces glowed with happiness. He looked away for a very long time. When he looked back, he said, "Surely this was meant to be."

So, Zipporah and the prince were married and lived happily ever after in a castle built just for them.

About This Tale

The black and beautiful Zipporah has a mean witch for a stepmother and a black, giant *djinn* (instead of a fairy godmother). After meeting the prince at a ball, she loses one of her boots in a rush to get home. Yes, here is a Jewish Cinderella tale from the Sephardim. As in many folktales, the good and the mistreated win over the bad and the selfish. The universal appeal of this tale type is remarkable. Well over 700 *Cinderella* tales have been recorded from nearly every culture.

The Israel Folktale Archives provided the source for "Zipporah and the Seven Walnuts." The Sephardim of Morocco shared this Cinderella variant. Many Jews who left their homeland during the Inquisition fled to Morocco because of its proximity to Spain.

The Contrarian

A shepherd named Murat lived with his family in the dry country we know today as Jordan. He and his brother raised sheep where the land with its sparse grass was only good enough for grazing. Life was peaceful as long as they avoided Bedouin herders who forced them off the best grazing spots. Murat's brother would say, "The dear Lord blessed us with health, work, and family, and that is good." For him, life was full.

But for Murat life was not full. As long as he could remember, he had one wish—to live in Jerusalem, the City of David. Each night he would dream the same dream. He had dreamed it so many times, the dream was like an old friend.

He saw himself walking in *Eretz Yisra'el*, the land of Israel, with a joyous smile, his greatest hope fulfilled. But one night the dream was interrupted. This time, an old man with a shining face stopped to speak with him. "Murat, it is time to go home. *Et dodim higi'ah: it is time to come closer to God.* Too shocked to speak, Murat wondered if it could be true, that he would see the land of his fathers! As the old man turned to leave, Murat begged, "Good sir, do not go. I have many questions. Is it true? Will I be so blessed to see the City of David? Tell me, by what path should I go?" Before disappearing the old man replied,

"Help will find you along the way."

Murat sat up in his bed, wide awake.

Although it was not yet dawn, he began preparations for the trip. He finished his chores, reminded his nephew how to avoid Bedouin herders, collected his few possessions, and was ready to bid the family farewell before the sun had set. His brother failed to convince him to wait until the entire family could travel together. "I do not like that you travel alone, but if you must go now, I wish you well." He placed as many coins as he could spare in Murat's hand and gave him his finest sheepskin quilt. "For the cold nights on the road."

His brother's wife made sure Murat had food and water. She gave him a goatskin water pouch fat with water. "Water will be scarce. Drink it wisely."

His nephew gave him a Magen David, a Star of David, carved from a sheep's bone. "To remind you where you are going."

∞

Murat walked through the night and by daybreak sat at the side of the road to rest. He wasn't sure he had taken the right path. *Eretz Yisra'el* was to the west, so Murat knew to walk away from the morning sun. Still, he wondered if there might be a better path to Jerusalem.

This was when he met another walker. Murat looked up to see an old man. He had appeared without a sound. The old man smiled at Murat and said, "Greetings, traveler! The month of May is going out and April is coming in."

What kind of greeting is this? thought Murat. *This old man is more confused than I am.*

"My name is Tarken," said the stranger with a smile. "I am here to see you reach home."

"How do you know where I am headed?"

"Last night in my dream I was told to find you and guide you home."

"Ah, yes, the man with the shining face. He told me that help would find me on my way."

Tarken shrugged. "I know of no shining face, only that I am here to guide you."

Murat shared food and drink with the stranger and before long they were talking like old friends. For some reason Tarken's presence made Murat feel safe. The stranger's voice, soft as a lullaby, calmed him.

As they were about to resume their journey, Murat had to turn the old man around so he would not walk to the East—away from their destination.

They walked until the clouds covered the sun and a strong cold, wind began to blow. The dust crept into their clothes and scraped their faces. Tarken blew on his hands to keep them warm, then placed them under his arms to avoid the cold. But once the wind stopped, the old man rubbed his hands together to warm them.

"We need a fire to take away the chill," Murat said. When the fire burned well, Murat noticed that this time, Tarken blew on his hands to cool them off, then placed them under his arms, to avoid the heat.

Murat shared his food and drink. Again, they talked as old friends, and again Murat wondered about Tarken. A nice man, so easy to be with, but what kind of a guide could he be? He got directions mixed up, did not know what month it was, and could not decide if his hands were too cold or too hot.

"Tell me," asked Murat, "is this the best way to Jerusalem? How do you know we are on the best route to the West?"

"Oh, not the west. We travel to the East!"

"East? Why east when Jerusalem is surely west of here?"

"True, but everyone knows that continuing to travel to the East will bring you to the West."

"I have heard this, but how can it possibly be so?"

"This for that; that for this! It is worth a try, don't you agree?"

Murat did not agree. It made no sense to him. He made up his mind to break away from this stranger and travel alone. "Tarken, please come away from the fire. I must speak with you."

Murat closed his eyes, took a deep breath, and reached for words that would rid him of this stranger without being unkind. With his eyes closed, he suddenly saw the man in his dream—the man with the shining face. The man

did not speak, only gazed directly at Murat with a questioning look. When
Murat opened his eyes, he looked long and hard at Tarken and could only say,
"Tarken, my friend, we must be on our way."

They walked until dark when, tired and thirsty, they stopped for the night.
Too tired to eat, they each took a long drink from the goatskin pouch before
resting by the side of the road. The old man fell asleep the minute he lay down.
Murat covered him with the sheepskin quilt and soon he, too, slept a deep and
dreamless sleep.

At daybreak Murat heard something. He jumped up to see a robber
drinking from the goatskin water pouch. Realizing he had been discovered, the
robber ran off. Quickly, Murat looked through their things. He found all the
food gone, and the goatskin water pouch on the ground nearby, empty except
for a few drops of water. All they had left was the sheepskin quilt, the empty
water pouch, the coins in one of Murat's pockets, and the Magen David in the
other.

Saddened, they started off once again. Murat thought, *With no water and
no food, how can we possibly get to Jerusalem?*

"Do not despair! This is the best news!" said Tarken. "Don't you know that
downs are followed by ups; ups are followed by downs? We are about to have
some good luck!"

"Tarken, Tarken," moaned Murat. "Please stop. Don't you see? We have no
water? We have no food?"

"Let me see that goatskin water pouch." As Tarken held the pouch, it grew
heavy—too heavy to be empty.

Murat checked the pouch to find it full of cool, clear water! "I don't know
how this can be, but I welcome it with a grateful heart." They took long drinks
and danced a little dance around each other. Refreshed, they set out feeling
more determined than ever to find Jerusalem.

They walked for hours. Both lunch and dinnertime came and left without a
bite of food. In spite of pangs of hunger they walked and walked. Finally, they
stopped to rest and to drink.

Soon they saw a woman walking toward them.

Murat offered her a drink from the goatskin water pouch and asked where she was headed.

After one long drink, she looked questioningly at Murat who nodded that she could drink again. "I walk to the inn where they buy my bread, and I offer you a loaf in thanks for this cool drink." They ate gratefully.

The woman told them the inn was about one hour away. "It's a good place, sirs. The innkeeper pays a fair price for my bread."

The three reached the inn at sundown. Murat used a few of the coins his brother had given him to buy dinner and a good night's rest indoors for himself and Tarken.

The next morning Murat asked the innkeeper for directions.

"Do we go west on this road to Jerusalem?"

The innkeeper laughed. "To get to Jerusalem, you best travel north before you travel west." He suggested they follow the road until they came to a fork. "There, you take the west fork to the river. Once you find the river, follow it with all its turnings until you come to the crossing place. For a small fee, the boatman will take you across. Once across, you will soon be in Jerusalem."

"Excellent!" shouted Murat. "How long will it take?"

The innkeeper gazed at the sky for a minute. "On foot, if you don't tarry, I think it will take at least one week to reach the river and another to the crossing place."

"Two weeks!" groaned Murat.

"I have a donkey you could buy to ease the journey. You can take turns riding, it will carry all your gear, and you will arrive much sooner."

Murat knew a donkey would be a great advantage. But there were only a few coins left, not enough to buy a donkey.

"I can offer you this sheepskin quilt from one of my brother's best sheep."

Surprisingly, this proved satisfactory. Once Murat saw the donkey, he understood why. Standing still, the donkey looked too tired to move, but once encouraged to walk, it stomped and brayed, stomped and brayed in protest. The innkeeper laughed. "Not to worry. A sound beating is all that it needs. Once it gets started, the beast behaves beautifully." The innkeeper gave them a generous supply of food for the few coins left in Murat's pocket.

When they wanted to start on the road again, the donkey would not move. Murat was angry. He shouted in a loud, mean voice, "You lazy beast! Move! You are good for nothing if you don't move. Move!"

But Tarken stroked the beast gently and spoke in a soft, sweet voice, "You just rest, my four-legged friend. No need to tire yourself. Just stay here and nibble on the grass." To Murat's surprise, the donkey began to walk.

At first both men walked beside the beast with Tarken's caressing voice encouraging it to stop, to rest easy. Then they took turns riding, and finally, Murat insisted the old man ride. From time to time the donkey would stop. It would stomp and bray, stomp and bray until Murat gave it a drink from the goatskin pouch and Tarken spoke soft words: "Yes, kind beast, stop this journey. Do not take another step." Then, satisfied as can be, it continued to walk. After several days they reached the fork in the road that turned west. Here was the longest part of the journey—to find the river. And, once they reached it, the river made so many turns that Murat was not sure what direction they were going. They ate very little to make the food last. Miraculously, the goatskin water pouch never went dry.

At last, they reached the crossing place.

It wasn't until they approached the boatman that Murat realized his few coins would not be enough to pay for the crossing.

"What is this?" asked the boatman. "A flea-bitten donkey and two travelers who don't look much better? That will be three fares, you know. The donkey doesn't ride free. We will have to use the barge. Crossing on my barge costs more than in my boat."

Murat's eyes widened. Of course, the donkey!

He convinced the boatman to trade two fares for the donkey. "My son, who lives on the other side, could use a donkey," admitted the boatman, "even one as worn out as this."

They all boarded the barge: the boatman, Murat, Tarken, and the donkey. They had crossed more than halfway when a storm approached. The wind swept them about; the rain came hard and fast. The donkey started to stomp and bray, stomp and bray. Tarken could do nothing to calm the frightened beast.

The barge wavered like a stick caught in a fast-moving stream. With the wildest look in its eyes, the beast stretched his head up and down as it stomped and brayed, stomped and brayed.

"Calm the beast! It will sink us for sure!" shouted the boatman.

And sink it did! They all tumbled into the boiling river, struggling to swim. Murat did his best to keep Tarken afloat.

By some miracle, they all managed to reach the shore, even the donkey.

"Are you all right, Tarken? I have never felt such a fright. We could have drowned."

"But we lived! And here you are in *Eretz Yisra'el*! You are only a short distance from Jerusalem. My work is done." Before Murat could thank him, Tarken disappeared as quickly as he had appeared when their journey began.

The boatman shouted, "Look at this! My barge is destroyed!" Walking away, he spat out some nasty words, ending with, "I never want to see you or your horrid donkey again."

Murat burst into tears of joy. At last he was in *Eretz Yisra'el*! Then, his laughter mixed with his tears. He couldn't stop laughing. Tarken was right! "Downs are followed by ups and ups by downs." He reached into his pocket and pulled out the Magen David. He gave it a kiss, mounted the donkey, and rode off toward Jerusalem.

About This Tale

This is one of many *aliyah* (literally, "to go up") tales—to return to live in the land of Israel. Known as ascension tales, they typically involve a dream or a heavenly voice that advises, "Come home." Since ancient times, Jews have shared a deep yearning to return. God promised this land to Abraham and his descendants as an everlasting possession. In the 6th century B.C.E., the Babylonians expelled the Jewish people from their land and destroyed their Temple. Later, in 70 C.E., the Jews were forced to flee or become slaves to the Romans, who defiled the Second Temple. Remembering that the Promised Land sustained the Jews through centuries of life in the Diaspora, they lived in foreign lands where, mistreated and misunderstood, they struggled to survive. Often, even when able to fit in peacefully, a strong sense of loss and homelessness prevailed.

Our tale takes place in the area we now know as Jordan. Murat, a simple shepherd, hopes to make *aliyah* someday. A dream of an old man with a shining face summons him to "return home." When he joyfully sets out on his way, he encounters a rather mixed-up companion—the prophet Elijah disguised as the Contrarian.

This tale grew from several different sources. The idea that "ups in life are followed by downs, and downs by ups" comes from a tale found at the Israel Folktale Archives. Volume four of *The Oriental Tales of Wisdom*[16] provided another source, "The Two Contraries." Here, a man invites a boy into his home. The boy can't make up his mind— first he is hot, then cold, then hot again. While his host wants to help the boy, he also wants to throw the boy out of the house for being so contrary. Still another source is the Judeo-Spanish ballad that reworks the lyrics to "May Song," a traditional song that welcomes springtime: "The month of May is going out and April is coming in." This backward version of the song was found in Armistead and Silverman.[17]

The Color Red

Long ago in the land called Yemen, there lived a Jewish family—a father, a mother, a son, and a daughter. In those days, the imam, the Muslim ruler, proclaimed laws for the Jews that made life hard. They were required to stand up in the presence of a non-Jew. They could not look directly into the eyes of a non-Jew, raise their voices as they spoke to them, nor brush against a non-Jew as they passed on their way. Because they could not build buildings higher than those of non-Jews, they built synagogues over a big hole—a space so deep that when they walked down into it, they could look up, up toward heaven.

And—they could not wear bright-colored clothing.

But these hard rules did not keep the Jews from their faith. Most were skilled craftsmen who studied Torah as they worked. Their skills were so great that non-Jews prized their products.

∽

Moshe, the father of this family, was a weaver. Nearly every fine lady and gentleman in the town wore clothing made of his weavings. The son, Reuven, spent each workday at his uncle's house. There his uncle taught him and another young man to make silver jewelry. Zorah, the mother, was a potter. She taught the daughter, Ruti, how to shape pots and fire them. Ruti also helped her father in his weaving workshop. She tended the snails, which were used to make a beautiful blue-colored dye for the tzitzit (the fringes) of the tallit (the prayer shawl). She spun wool and helped string the looms.

This story is about Ruti.

"She's a true beauty," her father would say, "and growing more beautiful each day."

"Yes," agreed her mother.

"But she should be married already! She's fifteen—nearly an old maid!"

"Yes," agreed her mother.

And with a fierce-looking face, he added, "I should never have let you talk me out of promising her to Avigdor, the printer. He would have been a good provider."

"Yes, Moshe, but he was too old for her, a widower with three small children. Ruti would not have it."

"Ruti would not have it! Ruti would not have it!" he shouted. "Wait until she marries. A husband won't put up with her independent ways. We have been too soft with her. You know, Avigdor would not give up. For months after I said no, he would ask me for her hand. Now, I hear he is to marry the widow Yona."

"Don't worry, Moshe. There is still time to make a good match." They looked at each other with serious faces, then smiled. They both wanted for Ruti what they had—a marriage full of love.

"Where is she?" he asked, using his rough voice once again. "Shouldn't she be helping you get ready for *Shabbat*?"

"She's making flowers out of scraps of colorful yarns for the *Shabbat* dinner table. Reuven is bringing a friend. 'If we can't wear colorful clothes,' she told me, 'we can at least have a few colorful flowers on the table for our *Shabbat* guest.'"

After dinner, Zorah and Ruti cleared the table as the men sang.

"Ruti, what do you think of your brother's friend Chaim? He was so quiet.

Maybe he has not a thought in his head."

"Or maybe he is shy, Mama."

"I saw you looking at each other. This isn't the first time you saw him, is it?"

"I see him when I go to Uncle's. Uncle says Chaim is a true artist who can fashion the silver as cleverly as Uncle does."

"And, what do you think of Chaim, my Ruti?"

"Me? I think he is very nice."

"And, what does he think of you, my Ruti?"

"He thinks I am very nice."

"I see," said Zorah as she gave her daughter a hug.

∽

When Zora and Ruti brought coffee for the men, Moshe invited the women to join them. Reuven was talking about a special bracelet Chaim had made. "Avigdor ordered a very fine silver bracelet for his bride-to-be. So Chaim designed one that Uncle says is the finest he's ever seen. But Avigdor canceled the order. He said it was too fancy for the woman he is now going to marry. When Chaim made the bracelet anyway, Uncle got angry because he said no one could afford it. Set in the center is a precious stone surrounded by letters forming the word "ARGAMAN," the first letters of the five angels: Ariel, Raphael, Gabriel, Michael, and Nuriel. The stone is an opal, which Chaim added after Avigdor canceled his order. And what an opal! It shimmers with every color of the rainbow. Uncle says it is the finest he has ever seen. When Uncle asked Chaim who could afford such a bracelet, Chaim said it was not for sale. The opal belonged to his mother. He plans to work off the cost of the silver."

Everyone looked at Chaim.

Chaim looked at Ruti.

Then Chaim turned to Moshe and said, "Sir, may I speak to you? Perhaps outside?"

When they left, Reuven told his mother and sister that Chaim designed the bracelet for his own bride-to-be.

"And who might that be?" asked Zorah.

"Perhaps we will know that soon," said Reuven. He looked at Ruti, who felt the color red on her cheek.

∽

For months it was a house busy with preparations for Ruti's wedding. Zorah was pleased her daughter had found a young man she loved and who loved her. Everyone respected him for his skill. At first, Moshe did not approve. "This young man is starting out in debt! It will take him a long time to pay for that bracelet. How will they live?"

"They'll manage, Moshe," said Zorah. "Just watch their faces when they look at each other. They'll manage."

Ruti spent time arranging a gift for her husband-to-be, a tallit. She prepared two sets of wool for her father to weave into the large square prayer shawl—one set from the finest black sheep and one the finest white sheep. *This will keep him warm on cold days,* she thought, *and it will be useful to carry things, too.* She paid particular attention to the blue dye for the tallit's tzitzit.

Moshe was busy weaving material for one of his best customers, a non-Jew who ordered fine red cloth for his daughter's wedding dress. After dying the wool, Ruti helped spin it into yarn and wind it into skeins that her father wove into a shimmering, ruby red cloth. She sat near the loom watching the red cloth take shape.

Oh, how Ruti wished she could be married in a dress made of this beautiful red color! It would show Chaim and the whole world how happy she was. Suddenly, she felt sad and angry all at once. *It is not fair that we cannot wear bright colors!* she thought. *What is the harm in it? A Jew is no different from a non-Jew! I* will *wear red for my wedding!* She was determined to ask her father. *After all,* she thought, *hasn't he always let me have what I want, once he understands how much it means to me? He'll speak in his loud voice and look fierce, but surely he will let me have a red wedding dress.*

Pulling together all her courage, she asked her father if she could make her wedding dress of this red material. To her surprise, Moshe did not shout, speak in his loud voice, or look fierce.

"It is a beautiful red, perfect for a wedding dress," he agreed. "But, my daughter, you know very well it cannot be."

"Why, Papa? No one at the wedding would tell that we broke the law. What harm could come of it?" She began to cry.

"You have found a loving, skillful man to share your life, Ruti. Why do you cry?"

"I cry to be married in the color red! I cry for the color of my happiness! We are no different from non-Jews. We love bright colors, too."

"My daughter, listen carefully," he continued in a soft, gentle voice. "We **are** different. We are Jews. It is never easy to be a Jew, and here it is especially hard. We must be what we must be. Remember the story of Korach, who went before Moses with his two hundred and fifty followers all dressed in blue, the blue of the tzitzit. He challenged Moses by saying that if a blue fringe was a reminder of heaven, how much better it would be to have everyone dressed in blue. Korach did not understand that it was God's plan to separate some as different, as special. We are special and here it shows by our not wearing bright colors."

Ruti stopped her tears and could only say, "Yes, Papa."

∞

On Ruti's wedding day she wore a dress her father had woven from a special black cloth. He had embroidered his daughter's black wedding dress with dark brown and dark purple pomegranates, her black leggings with dark brown and dark purple stripes, her black headdress with one large dark brown and dark purple pomegranate. Reuven had made her a silver string with tiny silver bells that she tied around her forehead. In her henna-colored hands she carried one of her mother's finest pots filled with bunches of rue for good luck. On her arm, she wore her husband's gift, the special silver bracelet with "ARGAMAN" engraved around an opal that shimmered with all the colors of the rainbow.

And on that day Ruti showed the whole world how happy she was, for her father, who could never bear his daughter's sad face, had sewn her wedding dress with the brightest, happiest red thread he could make for her. The seams of her wedding gown matched the touch of red in her cheeks. Ruti was married in the color red, the color of her happiness.

About This Story

"The Color Red" tells of the Jews who lived in Yemen many years ago. It looks at one family living in a society that forced strict limitations upon Jewish life. In spite of this, they managed to have productive lives. The Jews of Yemen are known for their expert craftsmanship: weavers, potters, printers, embroiderers, and makers of fine jewelry.

Yemenite Jews prepared weeks in advance for wedding celebrations. Traditionally, the bride's hands and feet were bathed in henna, an orange dye that gave her skin a shimmering glow. It was the custom for the groom to give his bride a gift of jewelry, an impractical gift of love. The bride gave her groom a tallit, a prayer shawl, a gift of faith. It doubled as a practical gift when used as a blanket for warmth or as a wrapping for carrying firewood. A pomegranate design became a favorite in Yemenite crafts, largely because it was said that the pomegranate has 613 seeds, just as the 613 halakhot, the laws of the Talmud.

For this tale, I am indebted to Zipporah Greenfield—friend, storyteller, and singer. It was inspired by the black wedding dress, sewn together with red thread, that belonged to Zipporah's grandmother. Zipporah's family emigrated from Yemen to Palestine before World War I. They took many Jewish children with them to escape the Yemenite threat of conversion to Islam.

The Grateful Dead

Once, there was a young man named Awad who wanted to see the world. When he decided to leave home, his parents, who were very poor, had nothing to give him—nothing but a few wise words.

"My son," they said. "Always be a *ben adam* (a kind and good person). Work hard and remember: When you do a mitzvah you become a mitzvah." (When you do a good deed, you become a good person.)

Awad said farewell to his parents and started upon his way. Though his pockets were empty, his heart was full of anticipation for the places he would see and the people he would meet. He traveled far and wide. And just as his parents had advised him, he worked hard and was kind to everyone he met.

One day, he stopped to work in a village where the rabbi had recently died. The people there were angry because the rabbi had not paid his debts to them. They were so upset about the money he owed them that they refused to bury him. When Awad heard about this, he arranged for the rabbi's burial and paid the rabbi's debts. This took all the money he had earned.

Awad felt good about helping the dead rabbi. After all, he was a rabbi, a righteous man, a man to be respected. But Awad felt sad, too. He didn't want to stay in a town where the people were more respectful of their money than their rabbi, so he sat in the shade of a big tree thinking about what he could do and where he could go now that he was a pauper once again.

High on a branch of the tree that shaded the young man sat the ghost of the dead rabbi. *Oh, now this will never do,* thought the ghost. *Here is a righteous man, a true* ben adam. *What he did for me was a great mitzvah. He was kind and he was generous. But now that I'm dead, how can I thank him?*

Suddenly, a stranger with a shining face appeared on the branch next to the rabbi's ghost. "Go down and talk to the young man," the stranger said.

"How can I do that?" asked the ghost. "He can't see me and if he could, he'd be frightened of a ghost."

"I'll go with you. It will be fine, you'll see," said the stranger.

When they both stood before him, the young man did not see a ghost. He saw two men, one with a short beard and one with a long beard. They talked for a long time about how Awad wanted to see new places and meet new people.

The stranger with the long beard had a suggestion—Awad could see many new places if he sailed on the sea.

"Yes," agreed the rabbi's ghost, "working on a ship could take you all over the world."

The young man thought about this. He closed his eyes and imagined working on ship. The more he thought about it, the more he liked the idea. When he opened his eyes, the two strangers had disappeared, but now he knew what he wanted to do. He traveled to the nearest seaport and joined the crew of a ship.

They sailed far and wide. When they came to land Awad went ashore to look around. Watching the people, he noticed a young woman, who gave her cloak to a sickly old man. Awad was surprised that she would give away such a beautiful cloak covered with fine embroidery. He watched her walk on until she saw some children dancing in the street. When she danced with them, her bracelets sparkled in the sun and kept the rhythm of their dance. Soon he joined them—dancing and laughing. When the children began to run away, the young woman called after them. "Wait! I have something for you." She gave each of them one of her bracelets. As they danced away, she stood smiling. But when Awad looked closely, he thought he could see a secret sadness in her face.

It wasn't long before he realized that he loved the woman because she was kind to everyone. And, she loved Awad because he was kind to everyone. Soon they were married. Still, he never asked about the secret sadness he saw in her face.

When his ship was ready to leave, Awad and his new wife sailed away. But the young man's wife soon felt sick from the ship's movement. They decided to settle at the first place the ship stopped. Here Awad found work as a tailor. His wife made beautiful embroideries for him to sell. Each time a ship came to their port, the young man sold some of his wife's embroidery. Because they both worked hard, they were soon wealthy. After a time, they were blessed with three children. Their life was filled with contentment—pleasant days and nights side by side.

People who lived in their village knew that if ever trouble were to strike, the embroiderer and the tailor would help. Your cat was lost? The tailor would find it. Your purse was stolen? The embroiderer would lend you money. Your soup was weak? The tailor would put a fat bone in it. Your son was slow to learn? The embroiderer would teach him. Your cloak was torn? The tailor would mend it.

∞

Far away, a king looked at a beautiful piece of embroidery that a ship had brought to his land and recognized the artful design. It was the work of his daughter, the long-lost princess. (And now you know the reason for the secret sadness of Awad's wife. She was the long-lost princess, the daughter of this king, who had run away from her father because he had been unkind to her.)

Immediately, the king arranged for the princess to be kidnapped and returned to his land. "Go there!" the king commanded his general. "And don't come back without her!"

Once the king's ship came to Awad's land, the general and his men wasted no time in finding where the princess lived. They waited until Awad left his house, and then they descended upon the princess and her children, bound them, and took them away to their ship.

The young man heard shouting at the harbor, where he was selling his wife's embroideries to visiting ships. Awad thought he heard his wife's voice crying for help nearby. He called to her and ran toward one of the ships. The general's soldiers were forcing his family on board and he tried his hardest, but could not push passed the soldiers.

"Cry all you wish, Princess," he heard the general say. "Your cries will do no good. Your father, the king, commands that I return you to him and that I will do!"

So, that's her secret. My wife is a princess, thought Awad. He kept calling to her and his children long after he could no longer see them. He could do nothing but stand there and watch the ship sail away.

∞

With his family gone, the young man was so downhearted that he stopped work and stayed in his house day after day. The people in the village tried everything to console him. After all, he and his wife had been so kind to them. Now that Awad was sad, they wanted to find a way to help him. Perhaps a song would help? The young man loved to hear music. But when a group gathered in his house to sing for him, he didn't seem to hear.

Perhaps tasty *boreka*s (sweet cakes) fresh from the oven would help? Their aroma was so inviting that you could taste them even before taking a bite. But the young man just turned his head away and sighed.

Perhaps some children dancing? Well, this just made the young man feel worse, because he remembered that when he first saw his wife, she was dancing with children.

Nothing they could think of helped him, so finally the people in the village gave up and went home.

On the roof of Awad's house sat the old man with the shining face and the ghost of the rabbi who Awad had once helped. "Oh, now this will never do!" said the ghost. "How can we help this young man?

"Come," said the old man. "We'll go down to talk to him—we'll see."

The young man was surprised to see the two strangers he had met so long ago. After a long talk about Awad's troubles, the old man with the long beard suggested, "Do something different. It will lift your spirits. You might, for example, open a vegetable market."

"Why a vegetable market?" asked Awad.

"Because you'll never be hungry if you have a vegetable market," the old man answered.

"And," added the ghost of the rabbi, "it will give you pleasure to see that others are never hungry."

The young man gave this serious consideration. "I don't want to sell the few pieces of embroidery that my wife left," he said. "They're all I have to remember her. And I can't go back to tailoring. That would remind me of the pleasant evenings we sat together when she would embroider and I would tailor. Yes, I'll do something different. Why not be a green grocer?"

∞

Many months passed. Awad worked hard at selling vegetables and continued his many acts of kindness. Soon he was wealthier than ever. He had property and gold, but he missed his family so much that he no longer looked like a young man. And he felt a sadness that only his family could erase.

In time, the princess convinced her father, the king, to let her take the children to visit relatives in a far-off land. "But," said the king, "under no circumstances will you be permitted to leave the ship before reaching your destination." The king selected a captain for the ship who always obeyed orders and commanded him not to let the princess leave the ship until they had arrived.

Shortly after their trip had begun, the princess spoke reproachfully to the captain. "Why do you have no fresh vegetables on board this ship? I'm a princess and these are my children. We'll fall ill because you neglected to buy fresh vegetables! My father, the king, will punish you for this."

"Forgive me, Your Highness," said the captain. "I will stop at the next port and send my first mate to buy fresh vegetables for you."

Now the princess knew that they were sailing close to the port where she and the children had lived with her husband. "No, Captain!" she said. "I will buy the vegetables myself to be sure that they are fresh and healthful. I command you to let me see to this myself."

The captain remembered that he was not to allow the princess off the ship, but what could he do? The princess had given him an order. He always obeyed orders. After all, she was a princess. Everyone must obey a princess.

When the princess stepped off the ship with her children she went directly to Awad's vegetable market. She recognized her husband immediately, even though his once black hair was now white. As you can imagine, their hearts filled with happiness.

The captain could not get the princess and her children to come back to the ship. They looked so happy that he could not bring himself to force them to leave each other again. Unfortunately, when he returned to his homeland, the furious king put the captain in prison. Then the king himself set out to bring back his daughter and grandchildren.

When the king found them, his soldiers held them captive. The king then summoned Awad to his ship. "I understand that you have done well here. You have property and you have set aside a tidy sum of gold. What will you give me to release your family?"

Without a minute's hesitation, Awad said, "Take it all. Only give me back my wife and children."

The greedy king agreed.

Awad, his wife, and children were reunited happily. They had no property and they had no money, but they had each other. The people of the village celebrated the family's reunion with singing, dancing, and good food, including tasty *boreka*s fresh from the oven.

The ghost of the rabbi and his companion looked down on the scene approvingly from the branch of a nearby tree.

"Oh, now this will do very nicely," said the ghost.

"Yes, indeed," agreed his companion with the shining face.

About This Tale

Here again, Elijah appears, this time as an old man who intervenes to reward generosity and kindness. The prophet helps the rabbi's ghost repay a kindness performed by the young man. Both the ghost and the prophet watch over this young man through good times and bad.

Several dominant folktale types/motifs run through this tale, among them a wanderer who seeks his fortune, an abducted princess, captives, charity rewarded, and the return of the dead to give counsel.

"The Grateful Dead" grew from a tale found at the Israel Folktale Archives. A Moroccan Jew who had immigrated to Israel told it to the archive researchers. This version, while greatly expanded, stays close to the basic tale as it was recorded.

The Vengeful Queen

The castle was at rest. The cook and her scullery maids, the blacksmith and his hearth, the dog and her pups, the soldiers who were to watch through the night, even the king in his grave many years, all slept soundly, all but the queen.

The queen was at work. Her eyes, wide with candlelight, blinked constantly as she worked long into the night. What compelled the queen to work so late?

In a few days it would be her birthday. The special celebration warranted a new gown worthy of her beauty. But her tailor had failed miserably. "I should have had his head!" she shouted aloud to the empty room. "In order to get anything done right, why must I do it myself?"

With a too sweet voice, she continued, mocking the way the tailor had spoken. "You are so right, Your Highness. The gown I made is not worthy of you. Yes, the bodice fits too loosely. . . But for young Princess Aldina, Your Majesty will be pleased. I have found a fine white silk to match the smile she shares with everyone. Her gown will surely be worthy of her."

Then the queen spoke in her usual rough, demeaning voice. "No! No new gown for the princess! It is of little importance what she will wear!" Repeating the conversation she had with the tailor earlier that day, she continued, "Tailor, I want you to tell the villagers that the princess is slovenly—she will not keep her clothes or herself clean . . . What? Don't tell me otherwise. If I say she is slovenly, she is slovenly!" *Imagine,* she thought, *such impudence! A tailor correcting me, the queen!* With each stitch, her mouth moved as if chewing a bitter root, her face as if displaying its sour taste.

Among the many guests invited to the celebration was a neighbor, Count Olinos, a man as handsome as he was wealthy. The queen knew that her daughter Aldina was beautiful. And this displeased her greatly. *Surely,* she thought, *my gown will have the count's eyes on me, and not on that young snippet!*

Suddenly, a sound split apart the stillness of the night. A pure, sweet song crept into the room. The queen gazed out her window, but she saw only darkness and the moon upon the lake.

In the morning, she asked Princess Aldina about the song. "Who could have been singing so sweetly in the night?"

"I heard no song, my lady," said Aldina, averting her eyes. "Perhaps it was the song of the mermaid in the lake."

"I know of no mermaid in the lake!" the queen snapped.

During the next two nights the queen watched for the mermaid as she sat stitching. Each night she heard the song, but saw nothing. Each morning Aldina averted her eyes as she said, "I heard and saw nothing, my lady. But, as you know, mermaids are terribly shy."

On the third night, when the queen heard the song, she ran to her daughter's chamber.

"Awake, daughter, awake and listen! You will hear the pure, sweet song of the mermaid."

Her daughter listened. Without averting her eyes, she said, "No, not the song of the mermaid, my lady. It is Count Olinos singing of his pure, sweet love . . . for me."

"This can never be!" exclaimed the queen. "I will see the count dead before he marries you."

"Then see me dead as well, my lady, for I return his love."

The queen, *may ill befall her,* shouted for the guards. "Find the count and carry him and Aldina to the dungeon!" There the two lovers awaited execution.

When the deed was done, they were both buried in the garden.

Over time, the lovers grew into flowering bushes—she into a red rose and he into a red carnation.

The queen, *may ill befall her,* dug up the plants, cut off the blossoms, and tossed their petals to the wind.

The lovers became birds—she a dove and he a hawk.

The queen, *may ill befall her,* had them hunted down. She threw their bones into the sea.

The lovers became fish—she a perch and he a carp. The queen, *may ill befall her,* had them caught and brought to her. She ground their bones into a fine powder, which she buried under her doorstep.

The lovers changed once more. She became a serpent and he a scorpion.

When the queen's foot touched the doorstep, ill befell her. With the serpent's bite and the scorpion's sting the queen was dead.

Such was the fate of the vengeful queen.

About This Tale

This tale incorporates the folktale motifs of magic, tragic love, and reincarnation. Here we have a rather scary tale of a queen and an ill-fated young couple. The selfish, mean-spirited queen speaks ill of her beautiful daughter and continues to inflict harm upon the couple even after causing their deaths.

You may wonder how this story found its way into a collection of Jewish tales. It does not fit the view that Jewish folktales deal with the lives of Jews, real and imagined. *Halakhah* (Jewish law) forbids Jews to speak ill of others, let alone commit murder or disturb the dead. In spite of the fact that Jews are not immune to evil talk or evil deeds, the tale just doesn't "feel" Jewish. And yet I found this story among Sephardic ballads where the Ladino was originally printed in Hebrew letters. According to Armistead and Silverman, this tale is "one of the most widely known Hispanic ballads abundantly represented throughout Sephardic areas."[18] The popularity of this tale among Sephardim illustrates the influence of secular culture upon Jews of the Diaspora. Generations of life within Spain, a dominant culture of its time, had a strong impact upon Jewish nonreligious life. Reminiscent of stories of metamorphosis from the Roman poet Ovid, our tale illustrates the enduring impact of folktales of the Roman period upon the culture of Spain. It also represents "the traditional Hispanic longing for an art in which virtue and true love are rewarded and evil does not go unpunished."[19]

"The Vengeful Queen" grew out of the Hispanic ballad "El Conde Olinos" (Count Olinos). It appears in one of the chapbooks of Y. A. Yonā who collected Judeo-Spanish popular literature between 1891 and 1920.[20] This popular song appeared in numerous versions throughout lands bordering the Mediterranean Sea. My retelling most resembles a variant from Morocco.

Nahum Bibas

Nahum Bibas lived in a small village near Valencia. It was a poor village, but the Jews who lived there didn't feel poor. They felt thankful for what they had and grateful that both the Moors and the Christians let them live in peace.

During the day, Nahum taught school. In the evening, he studied to become a *hakham,* a rabbi. This was his greatest wish. He dreamed of the time when he would hear:

"Good day, Hakham Bibas."

"Explain this, please, Hakham Bibas."

"How are you today, Hakham Bibas?"

For years now he worked at his studies. His teacher, the venerable *hakham,* would say, "Soon, Nahum. When you are ready, you will take my place here. You have learned much, but there is more still for you to learn. Be patient."

But Nahum and patience were not well acquainted.

He liked to get an early start each morning to hear the birds sing and to see the wildflowers open to a new day. As he walked to school, he thought of his students. *Shmuel, what can I do for Shmuel, who only wants to stare at the sunbeams crossing his desk? And Vaaknin: I can't keep up with him. Already he knows everything I know.*

"Bibas, have you heard the news?" It was Salamon, the baker, standing in his doorway where the sweet smell of fresh baked bread spilled into the morning air. This was Nahum's favorite stop on the way to school. He and Salamon would munch on warm bread and talk of this and that.

Salamon always had busy hands. If he wasn't working the dough for bread, he was turning something over and over in his hand. Nahum wondered what he kept moving around in his hand. *Probably bread dough,* he thought.

"So, Bibas, what do you think of the news?"

"What news?"

"The great el Cid now fights against King Alphonso of Castile," said Salamon. "He fights *for* the Moors! Imagine, Bibas, he was Alphonso's greatest warrior, fighting *against* the Moors! Now he has turned around. And here's the news: he has conquered Valencia."

"That *is* news!"

"I hear el Cid has set up camp near the coast," continued Salamon. "They say his tent is made of gold, his horse is covered with gold cloth to match his own garb, and his men are vicious warriors."

All rumors, thought Nahum. Still, it was troubling news. "What could have turned el Cid around so?" he asked.

"It is said that when they quarreled, the king banished el Cid from Castile," Salamon explained. "This made el Cid so angry that he went right to his old enemies, the Moors, and asked to fight against the king!" Salamon shrugged his shoulders as he moved something in his hand over and over. "Who can understand the Christians and the Moors? As long as they leave us Jews alone, what does it matter?"

But Nahum knew that it did matter. He was full of worry. *How will this man of power treat the Jews? It is true the Moors have left us alone these past few years, but I hear the Christians in Castile push Jews to convert. El Cid is a Christian, after all. Are we in danger? Better talk to the hakham, and better do so today.*

With this news, Nahum had even less patience than usual. Once his students completed their morning lessons, he told them what to study for the next day and said, "Go home. Play outside. Enjoy the beauty of the day." The children lost no time leaving the classroom.

Neither did Nahum. He ran to the *hakham*'s house and pounded on the door. The *hakham*'s wife opened it and whispered, "Nahum Bibas, what is it that makes you pound the door so hard? The noise disturbs the men studying Torah. Why aren't you in *heder* (school)? Why aren't you teaching the children?"

"The children are fine. They are playing outdoors in *ha-Shem*'s holy sun and air. This is an emergency!" He pushed past the *hakham*'s wife.

Surprised, the men looked up; the *hakham* stood.

"Bibas, what is it? What brings you here at this time? Trouble at school? A child is sick?"

"There is a new ruler in Valencia. What shall we do?"

"Yes, we have heard. Calm yourself, Nahum." The *hakham* spoke sternly, yet with kindness. Nahum Bibas was the best student he ever had. One day he would make a good *hakham*, to be sure, but he must learn to control himself. His excitement always got everyone else upset.

"How will this ruler treat the Jews?" asked Nahum. "What will we do if we must leave here? Where will we go? How can we protect ourselves?"

"What do you think we should do about it?" asked the *hakham*.

"Well, I'm not sure"

"I'm not sure, either, Nahum. We will pray," said the *hakham*. "*Ha-Shem* will help us think of what do."

With prayers completed, everyone waited to hear what the *hakham* had to say. The *hakham* looked down at his hands and said nothing for what seemed a very long time. Only a birdsong broke the quiet that filled the room. When he looked up, the *hakham* said, "We must send an emissary with a gift to show our respect for el Cid. And best to do so before there is any trouble."

Everyone began to speak at once. Who should go to Valencia? It should be someone wise, someone clever, someone holy, someone unafraid to stand before one so powerful. Of course! All agreed it should be the *hakham*.

But the *hakham* insisted he was too old. "It should be Nahum Bibas," he said. "Nahum will soon take my place as *hakham*. He is clever; he is brave. Everyone will agree he is a *tzadik,* a righteous man. And, heaven knows, he has enough energy to face el Cid and his army. Nahum Bibas will see that el Cid knows we Jews want only to live in peace."

With that settled, they all felt better.

Until they remembered that they would need a gift to present to el Cid! Who in their poor village had something that el Cid could value, something that would demonstrate their sincerity?

"The problem of the gift we will have to consider later," said the *hakham*. "The sun sets soon. *Shabbat* is approaching. Go, return to your homes and let us pray that the problem of the gift will be solved after the Sabbath."

All during *Shabbat* Nahum and the people prayed to find a gift worthy of both el Cid and their need for peace. Much discussion followed *Havdalah,* the service that marks the end of the Sabbath. Moshe suggested his grandmother's candlesticks. "True, they are brass, not gold, but when shined one could hardly tell the difference."

The *hakham* thanked Moshe. "I agree your candlesticks are extraordinary, but, Moshe, I fear the great el Cid will find them ordinary."

Jimena offered her embroidered silk cloth for the *hallah*. "It was a wedding gift from my rich uncle who lives far off in the East."

"It is a treasure, I agree," said the *hakham*, "but, Jimena, el Cid would have no use for a cloth to cover the braided bread of *Shabbat*."

Labe, the carpenter, offered a box on which he had carefully carved fruits and flowers. It was made of cedar wood. "When opened, the aroma fills the air sweetly."

The *hakham* smiled. "Labe, you are a true artist. The carving is lifelike and most pleasing to the eye, but I fear an empty box would not be well received.

"Listen, everyone: Go home. Search your hearts and minds. Surely we can find something suitable for el Cid."

But everyone feared that nothing in the humble village would do.

∽

On the way to school the next morning, Nahum again shared bread with the baker. "I've been thinking. We don't need a gift for el Cid. He must be a practical man. He is so important that he must have received many gifts, so many that it just may be that gifts no longer hold any value for him. Anyway, I'm sure I could convince him that we Jews only want to be left alone."

"That could be, Bibas," said Salamon, moving something around in the palm of his hand. "One thing I know is this: someone who is hungry prizes a tiny piece of bread, but someone with a full stomach leaves a whole loaf uneaten."

Nahum thought about this throughout the school day. Right after school he knocked on the *hakham*'s door once more. "Let's not wait until we find a suitable gift. Let's go right away. A gift is really not necessary. I will convince el Cid we just want to be left in peace." He was surprised to hear the *hakham* laugh out loud at this idea.

"Oh, Nahum, Nahum, what a great deal you have yet to learn! Your impatience clouds your thinking. Slow down and think about it. You would not have a chance to convince anyone. El Cid would take one look at you, if you even got close enough for him to see you, and have his men take you off to prison before you could say a word. Approaching him with no gift would be an insult. Of course you must take a gift. One thing I know is this: those who have the most, never cease to want more. Yes, there must be a gift, a very special gift presented in a very special way."

The next morning when Nahum stopped at the baker's for some bread and some talk, again he noticed how Salamon kept turning something in the palm of his hand. "What is it that you keep in your hand, Salamon?"

"What? This? It's nothing, just a stone. It calms me to feel its warm smoothness in my hand." One look and Nahum knew it was not "just a stone." It was golden in color, but not gold. It was smooth and warm to the touch. It shined as if the sun lived inside it.

"Salamon!" said Nahum, turning it over in his palm. It fit his hand just so.

"I've never seen anything like this. Where did it come from?"

"My cousin Suleiman, the sailor, found it. He sails all over the sea to far-off lands. The last time he docked in Valencia, Suleiman gave the stone to me. He said it wasn't worth anything, but thought I might like it because it was pretty. He found the stone in a port as far to the east as you can sail. It was a place he called Smyna. He called the stone a name I can't remember and said it came from the lands far north of where his ship could go. Suleiman said a stone like this was nothing special in Smyna, unless it was perfectly clear. Then it would be priceless. This one is not clear. That's why he gave it to me. See? Hold it to the sun, Bibas, and you will see a tiny bug caught inside." Salamon showed Nahum how, when he rubbed the stone, it would move things about. "They call it the gem of the north, the sun gem. It is only a pretty stone."

No, this is something rare," said Nahum. "No one here knows of stones like this."

Nahum was late to school that day. He and Salamon woke the *hakham* to show him the stone—and to give him fresh bread to make up for such an early visit. "Perhaps this would be valued by el Cid?" asked Nahum.

The *hakham* was delighted. "Yes, I have read about this. It has many names: *chasmal* or *karabe, or anbor, amber.* To find it, one must go far to the east and north. If perfectly clear, it is of great value. Perhaps the tiny bug inside won't matter. Chances are this is one thing el Cid does not have. Yes, we have our gift for el Cid!"

Later that evening, the *hakham* called everyone together. He showed how the stone, once rubbed, would move light objects. He explained that some thought the amber stone's warmth and smoothness brought good luck and good health. "A small flaw keeps it from being precious. Still, that might just not matter because it is a thing of beauty."

"Now," said the *hakham,* "now we can use Labe's beautiful box. We'll fill it with fine sand and place the amber in it. This is a gift worthy of el Cid. Perhaps now he will think kindly of us Jews."

And so, preparations were made. The *hakham* coached Nahum about what to say and how to say it. "Please, for once in your life, be patient! Under no circumstances should you rush, speak loudly, or contradict el Cid. Insist that you alone can deliver it to el Cid's hands. When in front of el Cid, be calm and state our simple purpose: *We welcome el Cid to Valencia with this modest gift. We Jews only want to live in peace.*"

Nahum practiced saying it again and again.

"Describe the stone before he sees it, Nahum. Maybe he won't notice it has a flaw. Tell him of its beauty, its powers to move things, to bring good luck, and to bring good health. Then present the cedar box and let him find it within the sand. It will shimmer and shine. It will be quite impressive."

The cobbler made Nahum new boots; the tailor made him a new suit. And under the suit he wore a *tallit* that belonged to the *hakham*'s father. "May this prayer shawl wrap you in *ha-Shem*'s blessing and protect you."

And so, Nahum Bibas was off to the port of Valencia with the cedar box packed safely in his travel bag.

∞

El Cid's camp was even more luxurious than Salamon's description. The colorful dress of his soldiers and his tents sent Nahum's head swimming. Each time he was stopped by guards, he explained that he carried a valuable gift for el Cid that he alone must deliver. Passing several checkpoints, he finally reached el Cid's magnificent tent. Nahum thought that the tent poles really were made of gold, just as Salamon said.

The two guards who stood in front of the tent pushed Nahum aside. "Be gone, little man. No one enters here unless el Cid's vizier Senor Fernando says so."

When Nahum asked, "Who is this Senor Fernando?" the guards said, "No one you need concern yourself with. Now be gone!"

But, Nahum would not be gone. Forgetting the *hakham*'s warning to remain calm, he began to shout, "I *will* see el Cid. I *will* see el Cid!" The guards laughed. One guard picked Nahum up and tossed him away from the tent. Nahum did not laugh. He brushed himself off as best he could, walked back to the guards, and continued to shout at the top of his voice: "I *will* see el Cid. I *will*! I *will*!" Each time, the guards took turns tossing him away from the tent and each time Nahum got up and shouted again. Soon there was a crowd of soldiers laughing and watching as the guards tossed Nahum down over and over.

As this was going on, Nahum's travel bag rolled away from him. No one noticed when one of the soldiers in the crowd searched through the bag. He found the cedar box, opened it, and took the amber stone. After replacing the empty box in the bag, the soldier joined the crowd laughing at Nahum.

"What noise is this?" shouted a man who came out of the tent. Stop this noise at once!"

Nahum ran up to him and begged, "Senor Fernando, will you please help me see el Cid? I have a valuable gift for him. It brings good luck, it brings good health; it is a beautiful gemstone el Cid will be proud to own."

"I am not Senor Fernando, I am his aide. A gemstone gift from this dusty little man?"

"Think what you will of me, sir, but it is true what I say."

"Give it to me and I will see that el Cid gets it."

"I am bound to place it in el Cid's hands myself."

"Wait here then! And you, guards, stop the noise and stop tormenting the little man."

When the aide returned, he motioned for Nahum to enter.

Nahum brushed himself off as well as he could, picked up his travel bag, and walked proudly past the guards into the tent.

What he saw frightened him. Here was luxury beyond belief. Rugs and pillows and tapestries woven of threads Nahum had never seen. He was not at all sure the amber stone would be of interest to a man of this wealth.

Mustering as much bravery as he could, Nahum stood tall and walked proudly toward the man seated before him. His fine clothes were overshadowed by a wise, shining face. "Who are you?" he asked. "What is so important that you shout so?"

He took a deep breath and spoke slowly, just as he had practiced. "*My name is Nahum Bibas. Sir, el Cid, we welcome you to Valencia with this modest gift. We Jews only want to live in peace.*"

"I am not el Cid, I am Senor Fernando. Tell me, why should I let Nahum Bibas speak to el Cid?"

"I am commanded to place this gift into el Cid's hands and only his hands."

"And who has commanded this?"

"My *hakham*, Senor."

Senor Fernando's smile lit up his face. "Ah, a *hakham*! A wise man!"

"Yes, Senor, the wisest man I know."

"Then, Nahum Bibas, you shall speak to el Cid."

He led Nahum into another part of the tent that was even more elegant. This was where the great el Cid sat reading.

"What is this, Fernando? You bring me a dusty vagrant?"

Nahum glanced down at his clothes and tried again to dust off his boots and suit. Then he took a deep breath and spoke slowly, just as the *hakham* had taught him: "*We welcome el Cid to Valencia with this modest gift. We Jews only want to live in peace.*"

"Ah, a Jew. And what is this gift you speak of?"

Nahum reached into his travel bag and held up the cedar box. "For you, great sir, with our compliments." He remembered the *hakham*'s directions. He was to describe the stone before giving it to el Cid. "In this box you will find a gemstone with great powers. It brings good luck, it brings good health, it does great things, and it is a thing of beauty."

As el Cid held the box, he turned it about admiringly. "Very nice carvings!" When he opened it, he took a deep breath, "Ah, cedar wood, a lovely scent. What is this? Sand?"

"Look deeper, sir, to find the gemstone."

"Ah! A gemstone? How very nice." He moved his fingers around in the box and felt for the amber stone. "I find no gemstone here. What kind of joke is this? How dare you waste my valuable time. Arrest this man!"

Guards were taking Nahum away when Senor Fernando spoke up. "Sir, let me help you." The vizier spilled all the sand that was in the box onto the rug. And there, shining brightly, was an amber stone that seemed bigger and brighter than Salamon's.

Nahum stared at it in amazement!

"I will see that stone," said el Cid.

As el Cid held it up to the light, Nahum stopped breathing, sure that the small bug inside would reveal its little value. But, to his amazement, el Cid was impressed by its clarity. He handed it to the vizier. "What is this, Fernando? Gold is cold to the touch; this is warm. Gold shines on the outside; this shines from within."

"I've heard of this stone," said the vizier. "In the East it is called *anbor*. This is an exceptional one, so clear and pure. I understand it has certain powers?"

Nahum could hardly speak. "Yes, yes, sir," Nahum said, catching his breath. "It brings good luck and good health. It also moves objects. Let me show you." Nahum demonstrated how it could move light objects.

El Cid was delighted. "I have nothing to equal this! So, you say the Jews only want to live in peace?"

"Oh, yes, el Cid, if you please, sir."

"So be it! My thanks to your people for this precious gift."

As Nahum and Senor Fernando walked out of the tent, he asked, "How could it be? The stone I brought was smaller and not a clear gem. It had a small bug."

"Yes," said the vizier, "I know."

How could he know that, wondered Nahum?

Nahum thanked the vizier. "I thank you, sir, for helping me and for helping our village. Thank you more than I can say."

Once more, the vizier's face lit up. "*Hakham* Bibas, go in peace. Go in peace, *Hakham* Bibas!"

Nahum's eyes opened wide. "You called me *hakham*! How did you know?"

Senor Fernando walked back into the tent, a smile on his shining face.

When Nahum returned with the news, there was much joy in the village. The venerable *hakham* called everyone together to celebrate.

"My friends, we honor Nahum. I am proud to call this young man, my very best student, *Hakham: Hakham* Bibas!

Nahum remembered the vizier's shining face and smiled.

About This Tale

A poor village near Valencia, Spain, provides the setting for this tale at a time before the Inquisition. The Moors and the Castilians were at war, but for the Jews of Spain it was a time of comparative peace. Clear amber was a prized semiprecious stone that made its way east via trade routes.[21]

The term "el Cid," a title meaning "sir" or "lord," was a common term of respect used during this time. However, the el Cid of our tale was a real person in history as well as our story character. His real name was Rodrigo Diaz de Vivar, a nobleman and soldier, famous for the many victorious battles he fought for his king, Alphonso of Castile. El Cid fell out of favor with Alphonso, possibly because his fame was growing greater than the king's. Alphonso banished el Cid from his homeland. To everyone's surprise, the angry el Cid joined his former enemy, the Moors. It is said that when they eventually resolved their quarrel, el Cid returned to Castile to serve Alphonso once more.[22] The basis for this tale grew from several sources. One comes from the Talmud in which a Jew is robbed on his way to present a gift to the Roman emperor. When the robber replaces jewels with sand, the emperor condemns the Jew to death. One of his officers (Elijah in disguise) intervenes with the news that it is magic sand. He says the sand will act as it did when Abraham tossed sand at the enemy and it became arrows and spears.

Another source is a story found in Ginzberg's *Legends of the Jews*.[23] When a Jew is robbed on his way to present a gift to a ruler, the robber replaces the gift with dirt. Insulted, the ruler condemns the Jew to death. Elijah, disguised as a court official, suggests that the "dirt" is special, an explosive powder useful in wars. When this is found to be true, the Jew is saved.

My retelling changes the gift to amber, a semiprecious stone rare in the eastern Mediterranean area at that time. Amber was highly prized for its clarity. Today, an insect encased within a piece of amber increases its value, probably due to the role of such a gem in the book and film *Jurassic Park*.

The Body Parts

This is the story of two daughters, Asilah and Hanina.

Asilah was the sultan's only child, and he loved her dearly. It is true that he had hoped for a son to take his place as sultan. When no son was to be born, he thought, *If this is Allah's will, so be it*. Custom prevented a sultana from ruling. Still, the sultan knew his daughter could have been a great ruler. She was as smart as any prince. She could do sums faster than the sultan's mathematicians, and already she had memorized most of the *Qur'an*. Always dressed in bright colors, she spread joy throughout the palace by sharing a smile and a cheery word with everyone she met.

Then, one day, she fell ill. The sultan was worried. None of his physicians could find a cure for her. They tried herb teas and soups, hot baths and cool baths, sunshine and shade. Nothing helped. She remained pale and too weak to get out of bed.

∽

Hanina was the tailor's only child, and he loved her dearly. It is true that he, too, had hoped for a son. How sweet it would be to study Torah with a son, to work with a son by his side. When that was not to be, he thanked *ha-Shem* for a daughter like Hanina. Custom would not allow women to study Torah or to be a tailor, but she was as smart as any son, and already she could sew a seam as straight as her father.

Because Hanina's neighborhood was too poor to have a real *kenesa* (house of prayer), they met at the house of the *hakham,* the rabbi, to study Torah. Hanina would sit in the corner to listen as her father and the others read Torah to seek its meanings. Hanina could not join in the discussions, but with her mind, with her eyes and ears wide open, she had much to think about. On the way home from these meetings, she and her father would continue the discussion. The tailor was impressed to hear wisdom from one so young, and from a girl.

Hanina spread joy wherever she went. She liked to spend time in the woods where she would talk to the animals. People smiled when they saw her because at times, she seemed to be talking to herself.

One day while walking in the woods, she saw a lion and her cubs. She ran all the way home to tell her father what she had seen. Now Hanina thought with all her body parts. Her tongue blurted out, "Father, in the woods, I just saw a dog and its pups." The tailor smiled and said, "That's nice, dear." When she got excited, her tongue would say things like that. She would look at a cat and call it a mouse. She would look at a donkey and call it a sheep.

The tailor worried about this, but he did not know what to do. One day, he said, "Our *hakham* can answer the most puzzling questions. I'll ask him." The *hakham* listened to the tailor and said, "Don't worry about that one. Hanina is a bright girl. I can see her sitting in the corner when we study Torah. With her whole self, with all her body parts, she thinks. As long as her tongue speaks carefully, there is no need to worry. Caution her to mind her tongue. He who guards his tongue keeps troubles far away."

∽

Now the sultan was worried about the princess. "I must do something fast. I cannot let another day go by without finding a cure for her. He asked his trusted vizier, "What can I do? Who can help me?" The vizier scratched his head and pulled his beard until at last he had an idea. "I have heard of a very wise *hakham* who lives near the edge of town. Some say that he can find the answer to any puzzling question. Perhaps he could help."

"Bring him to me at once!" demanded the sultan.

That very day, the *hakham* stood before the sultan. When he heard about the princess and the many cures they had tried, he thought long and hard. He looked toward the heavens, then he looked at the king, and he looked toward the heavens again.

"Milk—" the *hakham* said, but he was only able to say this one word before the sultan, in his haste, interrupted him. "Ah, yes!" the sultan shouted. "We have tried everything but milk! Hurry, bring milk to the princess." Everyone rushed out of the throne room, leaving the *hakham* standing there alone. What could he do? He turned and went home.

The sultan's servants served the princess the milk of a cow. The princess drank it cold, she drank it hot, she drank it warm. She even took a bath in it. They waited, but still the princess was ill.

Then, they served her the milk of a goat. The princess drank it cold, she drank it hot, she drank it warm, and she bathed in it. They waited, but still the princess was ill.

The sultan sent for the *hakham* again. "We gave her milk and it did no good. What do you have to say for yourself?"

The *hakham* shook his head. "What do I have to say? I would like to finish what I had to say before. The princess will get well if she drinks MILK OF A LIONESS."

"Ah!" said the sultan, greatly worried. "Are any of my subjects brave enough to milk a lion?"

He called all his advisers together and asked who would get the milk of a lioness for the princess. No one would do it. His generals assembled the army in the courtyard so he could ask them. None of the soldiers would risk getting so close to a lion.

Now the sultan was extremely worried. "Surely there must be one brave man in my kingdom." He sent messengers throughout the land to announce that the man who would bring him the milk of a lioness would receive a great reward. The sultan would build him a new house and give him gold and silver for the rest of his life. "That ought to be enough to make a man brave!" he said. But he grew sadder and sadder, for no one answered his call.

∽

Hanina was on her way to the market when her eyes caught sight of one of the sultan's messengers. Her ears listened carefully to his message. The milk of a lion? Her mind thought of the lion she saw in the woods. Her feet walked her up to the messenger and her tongue began to speak in a very confident voice. "I am the tailor's daughter. I will bring lion's milk to the princess!"

The messenger laughed. "Go away, little girl. We are not playing at games here."

"But I will, I will!" shouted Hanina's tongue. "Tell the sultan not to worry. I will be there soon."

Each day, as his messengers returned to the palace, the sultan waited for news of some brave man to milk a lioness. And each day the sultan went back to the throne room sadder than the day before. The messengers hated to see his saddened face. That is why the messenger who had met Hanina finally spoke up. Even though he knew she could never do it, he told the sultan he had found one person who agreed to milk a lioness.

"At last!" shouted the sultan. "I knew I would find someone in my kingdom brave enough to help! Tell me the man's name."

"Well," stammered the messenger, "it's not exactly a man."

"Oh, a brave young boy, then. Who, who?"

"Yes, this is a young person, your highness, but I do not know the name."

"No matter," said the sultan. "When will this be done?"

"Soon, my master. 'Soon' was all this young person would say."

∽

The tailor knew nothing of his daughter's plan, for if he did, he would surely have stopped her. Early the next morning Hanina told him she was off for a walk in the woods.

"Be careful, Hanina."

"Of course, Papa, I'm always careful."

Hanina returned to the spot where she had seen the lion and her cubs. Her ears heard the lion moaning. Her eyes saw a big scratch on the lion's nose that looked very sore. When her feet began to walk up to the lion, she stopped and waited for her mind to think of a plan.

"I will come back with meat for you to eat," she said.

The lion growled angrily back at her.

Every day for a week, she took meat to the lion. Every day for a week she made sure her tongue spoke softly to the lion. At first she tossed the meat from a distance, but after a few days she began to move closer and closer, until at last she stood before the great beast. "Here, dear lion, I bring you a bowl of cool water from the stream to quench your thirst." As the lion drank, it stopped growling. Continuing softly, Hanina moved closer still. "That's right, Mrs. Lion. Drink it all." Once the water was gone, Hanina filled the bowl with a soothing medicine. She told the lion, as softly as possible, "Now, Mrs. Lion, dip your nose in this. It will help fix your nose."

Seeming to understand her, the lion first smelled the medicine, then rubbed its sore nose in it. The lion roared such a loud roar that Hanina jumped back. But when she looked, she was sure she saw the lion smiling. "Yes, after the first sting it helps, doesn't it?"

When Hanina returned the next day, she noticed the lion's nose was not as red and not as swollen. There was no more growling when the beast saw her. This time she walked right up to the lion and asked, "If you will be so kind, may I please have some of your milk for a very sick princess?" Since there was no roar or growl of protest, Hanina pushed aside one of the lion pups and milked a bowl full of milk. "I thank you, Mrs. Lion! The sultan and the princess thank you! We all thank you!"

On her way to the palace, Hanina could not contain herself. Something strange began to happen. Her body parts began to argue about who should take credit for getting the milk of a lioness.

"If it weren't for me," said Hanina's eyes, "you never would have seen the messenger and learned of the sultan's quest!"

"What do you mean?" shouted Hanina's feet. "We walked to the woods and found the lioness!"

"No, no!" said her ears. "I heard the sultan's announcement. I should get credit for the milk!"

Her tongue said nothing.

Once she reached the palace with the news, Hanina was ushered into the throne room where the sultan welcomed her. With great excitement, she said, "Here, o Great Sultan, here is what you need to cure the princess. Here is the milk of . . . a dog!"

Suddenly, the throne room grew quiet. "What? Do you mock me, child? Who are you and how do you dare approach me with the milk of a dog? Arrest her! Take her out of my sight!"

Guards carried her off to the dungeon.

When the tailor heard what had happened he ran to ask the *hakham*'s advice. "What can I do? How can I help my daughter?"

"Come!" the *hakham* said. "We will go. We will see. We will try."

At the jail, the tailor asked, "Hanina, my dear child, is it true? How could you do this? Tell me what happened."

Now, Hanina's tongue was feeling very badly for speaking incorrectly from excitement. To make up for it now, her tongue explained everything and assured the tailor that the milk really was the milk of a lioness.

"Hanina, Hanina," the *hakham* said, shaking his head, "you must remember: He who guards his tongue keeps trouble far away."

The *hakham* and the tailor begged the guards to see the sultan. "Go away!" they were told. "The sultan will see no one—certainly not you two!"

The tailor would not stop begging to see the sultan, so the guards took him to the vizier. "Do not expect mercy," said the vizier. "There can be no mercy for someone who would trick the sultan in this way." The tailor spoke fast. He explained how Hanina got things mixed up when she was excited. "Please, I beg you, test the milk to see if it is, indeed, the milk of a lioness."

"Go home. No one believes a young girl could milk a lioness. She told a wild tale. There is nothing you can do for your daughter."

Then, the *hakham* spoke. "Wait just a minute, sir. Think of this: What if it is not a wild tale? What if it truly is the milk of a lion? What if you are responsible for keeping the cure from the princess? What then?"

"All right, all right! We'll test the milk."

Once the princess had a spoonful of lion's milk, she began to feel better. The sultan's physicians gave her one spoonful every hour. When it was all gone, she slept for three days. On the fourth day, she jumped out of bed and into the sultan's arms, as healthy and happy as ever.

True to his word, the sultan rewarded Hanina with a fine new house and enough gold and silver to last her a lifetime. He appointed both Hanina and her father his royal tailors. One of the first things Hanina did with her new wealth was to build a *kenesa* for her neighborhood. From that time forward, the *hakham* said, they would bend custom and permit Hanina to join in the study of Torah.

As the years went by, Asilah was honored for her wisdom and kindness. The sultan kept her by his side because he respected her advice above all others. When the sultan grew too old to rule, he made a proclamation. From that time forward, he would bend custom and permit a woman to rule the land.

About This Tale

"The Body Parts" combines two tales: "The Milk of a Lioness" and "The Conflict Between the Limbs." Both reveal a survival technique used by Jews—exaggerated tales of Jewish bravery or intelligence. A tale of a Jew fearlessly milking a lioness could give a sense of control and power to the powerless. Keeping control of what your tongue says and where your body parts take you could save your life.

This was a time when the rabbi not only guided his people spiritually, he advised them in all things. In our tale, a rabbi's advice and knowledge are so well known that a sultan seeks his counsel. Jews could feel a strong sense of pride with a story that has a sultan asking advice from a rabbi.

This tale incorporates several common folktale types/motifs, for example, an extraordinary illness, a grateful animal, and fathers and daughters.

The tales I combined to create "The Body Parts" came from Jews living in the Muslim lands of Syria and Morocco, recorded at the Israel Folktale Archives. Our story also has ties to the ancient tale, "Androcles and the Lion."

The Ivory Flute

It was springtime when all things seem possible.

Count Alemare set out with his army of 10,000 men to battle the French. He felt sure he would return to find fame and fortune.

They had been on their journey many days when Alemare heard of a country fair nearby with lively entertainments. Because he knew a happy, rested army fights stronger than an unhappy, tired one, he decided to make camp near the fair. The food, the jesters, and the dancing pleased them all.

It was at the fair that Alemare first saw the ivory flute. One glimpse and he knew he must have it. The flute was resting on top of a pile of carpets in a merchant's booth. The creamy white ivory with its delicate carvings of triangles made into six pointed stars shimmered in the sunlight. *How sweet the sound will be,* thought Alemare, *when I play such a flute as this!* The merchant, who had a red beard, said he did not want to sell it, but when Alemare took 100 gold pieces from his money pouch, the flute was his.

As soon as he reached his tent, Alemare blew into the flute to play a tune. *What is this?* he wondered. Not a sound came out. Perhaps he needed to blow harder. He tried again and again, to no avail. He asked Ramon, his first adviser, to try; he asked the soldier who blew the horn to alert the troops to try; he asked his lieutenants and his captains. All failed to make a sound.

"Curses upon this flute!" he shouted. "I can't believe I gave one hundred gold pieces for a flute that is mute!" He commanded Ramon to return the flute to the merchant with a red beard. "Take it out of my sight. Demand the return of my hundred gold pieces. I will not be tricked like this!"

Ramon and his servant, a Jew named Nesim, set off for the fair. While Ramon watched the dancing ladies and ate sweets, Nesim looked for the carpet booth and the man with a red beard.

∞

Soon Ramon returned to the count with the bad news: the carpet merchant with a red beard was no longer there and no one knew of his whereabouts.

"Go back to the fair," commanded Alemare. "Hear me, Ramon, I will have your head if you return without my gold."

Back at the fair, Ramon sent his servant Nesim out again. Nesim looked once more, but it did no good.

"It is no use, sir," Nesim told Ramon. "The red-bearded merchant is gone."

"What am I to do? Count Alemare will have my head if I don't return with a hundred gold pieces. Think, Nesim, think!"

"Why not try to sell the flute, sir? It is a beautiful thing. Maybe someone will want it just for its beauty."

"Yes," Ramon said, "you must sell it. Stop only people who look as though they might have a hundred gold pieces. Talk to them of its beauty. Surely someone will want to buy it just as the count did."

Nesim stopped and talked to many people who looked wealthy enough to buy the flute. They agreed it was a thing of beauty. However, once told the price for a flute that made no sound, they merely laughed and walked away.

When Nesim returned with the flute, Ramon grabbed it. "I can see I will have to do this myself!" After three or four unsuccessful talks with people who were well dressed, Ramon stopped looking for wealthy people and started to talk to anyone who would listen to him. "I'll take fifty gold pieces, twenty-five gold pieces!" But no one wanted a silent flute.

Ramon knew he could never return to camp without one 100 gold pieces. "If I could, I'd pay for it myself and toss this flute into the river! But I don't have one hundred gold pieces." Count Alemare's parting words haunted him: *"Hear me, Ramon, I will have your head if you return without my gold!"*

Ramon decided the only thing for him to do was to run away. As he tossed the flute to Nesim, he said, "Tell the count that thieves set upon us, took the flute, and killed me. Tell him anything! I cannot return."

"But, sir!" shouted Nesim. "Wait! What am I to do?" He watched Ramon walk away in a direction far from the army's campground. It was the last time Nesim saw Ramon.

Now, Nesim knew that if he returned to camp with the silent flute and no gold, the count would surely have his head instead of Ramon's. He sat down on a rock to think. And think he did—long and hard. *I cannot return and tell the count the lies Ramon asked me to tell. And, I cannot return and tell the count the truth: that Ramon shamefully ran from his duty. Each of these goes against halakhah. I must complete Ramon's task. I must either return with the man who sold the flute to the count, or sell the flute and return with 100 gold pieces.*

∽

For many months Nesim traveled to every bazaar and market he could find. No one had heard of the carpet merchant with a red beard, and no one wanted to buy the beautiful, but silent, ivory flute.

One day, as Nesim was stopping people to ask if they might buy the flute, he met a young man with a shining face. Because the young man wore dusty clothes and looked hungry, Nesim thought he would probably not have the gold to buy the flute.

"I hear you have a flute for sale," the young man said. "I have no gold, but may I look at it?" He held it gently and admired its beauty. "Would you mind if I play it, sir?"

Nesim looked at the young man and laughed so hard his eyes closed. "Play it! Yes, please play it," he said. He could not stop laughing until . . . what was this? He heard the most beautiful sound ever played! The young man could make music with this flute! And what music he made!

Nesim then felt something heavy in his pocket. He pulled out a pouch. Inside he found 100 pieces of gold! "Young man, tell me your name. Oh, never mind, just come with me. You must meet Count Alemare."

They traveled together for many weeks. When they got close to home, Nesim heard that Count Alemare and his men had fallen on bad luck. They had lost every battle; the French had driven them out, defeated. What's more, Count Alemare returned home to find such displeasure with his defeat that he had been imprisoned in the White Tower. This distressed Nesim greatly, for he knew that the White Tower held prisoners awaiting execution.

When at last they reached the White Tower, Nesim and the young man approached Count Alemare's cell. The count asked, "Who is this come to see my disgrace?"

"I am Nesim, servant to Ramon, your former first adviser."

"My former first adviser, Ramon? Whatever happened to him?"

"No matter, my count. I come with the hundred gold coins you commanded Ramon to fetch. And, also the ivory flute."

"That ivory flute! Don't mention it to me. All my bad luck started with that flute. Get it out of here!"

"Wait, my count. This young man can play the ivory flute."

The young man began to play and as he did every cell in the White Tower opened up, freeing all the prisoners. The young man continued to play the sweetest-sounding music the count had ever heard.

"Don't stop," begged the count. "Don't stop this marvel!" As the young man continued playing, birds sang and gathered overhead, which caused a pleasant shading from the hot sun. Enough fish leaped from the river to feed the entire town their supper. In houses of the wealthy and the poor, all items, long lost and nearly forgotten, were found. Crying babies yawned and slept soundly.

It was not long before Count Alemare collected his army and returned to France. He took Nesim and the young man with him. Each time the sound of the flute was heard, Alemare's enemies turned and ran away. Alemare won all his battles. Fame and fortune awaited him upon his return.

The count sent a messenger to fetch the flute player and Nesim. He wanted to reward Nesim for his loyalty and the young man for his ability to make the magical flute sing. When his messenger returned, only Nesim stood before Count Alemare.

"Where is the young man, the only one who can play the ivory flute?"

"He has gone, my count," said Nesim, "but before he left, he asked me to return your flute."

The count smiled as he held the flute. Thinking the spell was broken, that he just might be able to play it, the count blew into the flute several times. But, just as before, no sound came out. "Oh, well," he sighed, "I will keep it with me always, even though it remains silent. I will never forget its sweet sound and the magic it performed."

He then made Nesim his first adviser. And with the ivory flute and Nesim by his side, Count Alemare kept peace and prosperity throughout the land.

About This Tale

This story centers upon a beautiful but silent flute and a simple but honest Jew. En route to France with his army, Count Alemare spends a dear price for a flute that makes no sound. Angered by its silence, which calls attention to the count's arrogance and lack of humility, he commands his first adviser to retrieve his money or lose his life. Unable to do so, the first adviser deserts, leaving his servant, a Jew named Nesim, with the task. Rather than run away, Nesim continues the search. A very long time passes before Nesim finds the only person who can make the flute sing. And when it sings, the music makes magical things happen. Our friend, the prophet Elijah, makes another appearance in this tale. Disguised as a poor young man, he plays the flute to help a Jew who will not shirk his duty—a righteous Jew.

Y. A. Yoná's ballad chapbooks, collected by Armistead and Silverman, provided the source for this tale.[24] Yoná collected ballads from the Sephardic communities of Salonika, Greece, and Sofia, Bulgaria, and had them published in Ladino. "The Ivory Flute" grew out of one of these ballads, "El Chuflete" (The Magic Flute or Whistle).

Notes

1. The standard index of folktale types and motifs developed by Aarne and Thompson contains some 40,000 distinct motifs categorized for easy reference. The motif index is a six-volume guide to various motifs found in the literature of peoples throughout the world. See A. Aarne and S. Thompson, *The Types of Folktales* (Helsinki: Fellows Communications, 1973). The Israel Folktale Archives extends Aarne-Thompson with its own index devoted to Jewish folktales.

2. For an Ashkenazic Cinderella, see N. Jaffe, *The Way Meat Loves Salt* (New York: Henry Holt, 1998). For a Cinderella from the Sephardim, see "Zipporah and the Seven Walnuts" one of the stories in this collection. For more on the Cinderella motif, see *Cinderella: A Casebook,* ed. A. Dundes (New York: Wildman Press, 1983).

3. These two perspectives have been referred to as polygenesis and monogenesis theories in Z. Sutherland and M. H. Arbuthnot, *Children and Books* (New York: HarperCollins, 1991). The polygenesis theory holds that folktales evolve from numerous sources. It suggests that folktales express a deep emotional need common to all humans, thus the appearance of similar tale motifs throughout the world. Carl Jung is among those who have held this view. See his *Man and His Symbols* (New York: Dell, 1964). The monogenesis theory holds that all folktales emanate from one source. J. T. Bunce agrees, claiming that all tales come to us from ancient peoples of India and Iran who were called Aryans. See his *Fairy Tales: Their Origin and Meaning* (London: Macmillan and Company, 1878). In modern times the term "Aryan" has come to mean a Nordic-type Caucasian, supposedly part of a master race. It is interesting to note that Adolf Hitler was said to have been fascinated by German/Norse myths and hero tales and used them to help justify his claim of Aryan superiority in his establishment of a new German nationalism. See Christa Kamenetsky, "Folktale and Ideology of the Third Reich," *Journal of American Folklore,* 90:356 (Apr-Jun 1977): 168–178.

4. The differences revealed by Walter Ong when he compared oral and written thought show how well they complement each other. See Walter Ong, *Literacy and Orality* (Cambridge: Cambridge University Press, 1991).

Oral Thought	Written Thought
Situational	Abstract
Multidirectional	Linear
Immediate	Historical
Sound	Sight
Uses no tools	Uses pen/computer
Leaves no record	Leaves a record
A process	A product

5. Dov Noy, "The Jewish Versions of the 'Animal Languages' Folktale (AT 760): A Typological-Structural Study," *Scripta Hierosolymitana* 22 (1971): 171–208.

6. Dov Noy, *Folktales of Israel* (Chicago: University of Chicago Press, 1963).

7. The foundation sponsors a chat group, Ladinokomunita, that provides opportunities to speak and to hear Ladino spoken, as well as to learn the language, history, and culture of the Sephardim through course work. See http://www.sephardicstudies.org. or info@sephardicstudies.org.

8. See Matilda Koén-Sarano, *King Solomon and the Golden Fish* (Detroit, MI: Wayne State University Press, 2003).

9. Oicotype, according to Noy, is a term coined by Carl von Sydow in Noy (1971). The term refers to a local tale type found in a particular cultural area.

10. S. G. Armistead and J. H. Silverman, *The Judeo-Spanish Ballad Chapbooks of Yacob Abraham Yoná*, vol. 1 of *Folk Literature of Sephardic Jews* (Berkeley: University of California Press, 1971).

11. L. Ginzberg, *Legends of the Jews* (Philadelphia: The Jewish Publication Society, 1969), 275, 309.

12. R. Haboucha, "Types and Motifs of the Judeo-Spanish Folktales," in T*he Garland Folklore Library,* ed. A. Dundes (New York: Garland, 1992) and M. Koen-Sarano, *Folktales of Joha, Jewish Trickster,* trans. D. Herman (Philadelphia: The Jewish Publication Society, 2003).

13. G. W. Dennis, *Tzohar Encyclopedia Mythica* (2005), http://www.pantheon.org/articles/t/tsohar.html.

14. Ginzberg.

15. Armistead and Silverman, 241.

16. Ginzberg.

17. Armistead and Silverman, 353.

18. Ibid., 154.

19. Ibid., 170.

20. See Armistead and Silverman for more about el Cid and the numerous ballads and tales he inspired.

21. Ginzberg.

22. For more about the banishment of el Cid see Chris Lowney, *A Vanished World: Medieval Spain's Golden Age of Enlightenment* (New York: Simon & Shuster, 2005), 130.

23. Ginzberg, 203.

24. Armistead and Silverman, 352.

Bibliography

Aarne, A., and S. Thompson. *The Types of Folktales*. Helsinki: Fellows Communications, 1973.

Armistead, S. G. *Oral Literature of the Sephardic Jews*. http://flsj.ucdavis.edu/home/sjjs/orallit/litorale13 (accessed July 24, 2001).

Armistead, S. G., and J. H. Silverman. *The Judeo-Spanish Ballad Chapbooks of Yacob Abraham Yoná*, vol.1 of *Folk Literature of the Sephardic Jews*. Berkeley: University of California Press, 1971.

    Judeo-Spanish Ballads from Oral Tradition, I Epic Ballads, vol. 2 of *Folk Literature of the Sephardic Jews*. Berkeley: University of California Press, 1986.

    Judeo-Spanish Ballads from Oral Tradition, II Carolingian Ballads, 1: Roncesvalles, vol. 3 of *Folk Literature of the Sephardic Jews*. Berkeley: University of California Press, 1994.

Ausubel, N., ed. *A Treasury of Jewish Folklore*. New York: Crown, 1948.

Awam, Abdulsamad Salim ben. *The Untold History of Jews of Yemen*. http://www.wzo.org.il/en/resources/debate_subject (accessed July 25, 2005).

Baird, Rodney R. *History of Amber*. http://www.ancientroupe.com. (accessed February 22, 2006).

Bin Gorion, M. J., and Mimekor Yisrael. *Classical Jewish Folktales*. Vols. 3–4. Bloomington: Indiana University Press, 1976.

Bosma, Bette. *Fairy Tales, Fables, Legends and Myths*. New York: Teachers College Press, 1992.

Bunce, John Thackray. *Fairy Tales: Their Origins and Meaning*. London: Macmillan and Company, 1878.

Cheichel, Edna. *A Tale for Each Month, 1968–1969*. Edited by Dov Noy. Israel Folktale Archives Publication Series No. 26. Haifa, Israel: Haifa Municipality, 1970.

Conger, D. *Many Lands Many Stories*. Rutland, VT: Charles E. Tuttle, 1987.

Dennis, Geoffrey W. *Tzohar Encyclopedia Mythica*. http://www.pantheon.org/article/t/tsohar.html. (accessed November 14, 2005).

Dorson, Richard M, ed. *Folktales Told Around the World*. Chicago: University of Chicago Press, 1975.

Dundes, A. *Cinderella, a Case Book*. New York: Wildman Press, 1983.

Freedman, H., and M. Simon. *Midrash Rabbah*. 10 vols. London: Soncino Press, 1961.

Fried, E., ed. The Eternal Jewish Bride: A Survey of Jewish Marriage Customs.

http://www.torah.org//learning/women/class9.html+8hl=en (accessed September 20, 2005).

Ginzberg, L. *From Exodus to the Death of Moses,* vol. 3 of *Legends of the Jews.* Philadelphia: The Jewish Publication Society of America, 1969.

Goitein, S. D. *From the Land of Sheba.* New York: Schocken Books, 1973.

Greenberg, M. "The Stabilization of the Text of the Hebrew Bible Reviewed in Light of the Biblical Materials from the Judean Desert." *Journal of American Oriental Society* 76 (1956): 157–67.

Haboucha, Reginetta. *Types and Motifs of the Judeo-Spanish Folktales.* Edited by A. Dundes, vol. 6. *The Garland Folklore Library.* New York: Garland, 1992.

Hall, Rene. "The DNA of Fairy Tales: Their Origin and Meaning." *Sunrise Magazine* (August/September 2000).

Hansen-Roken, Galit, and D. Schulman. *Untying the Knot on Riddles and Other Enigmatic Modes.* New York: Oxford University Press, 1996.

Hansen-Roken, Galit, and Eli Yassif. "The Study of Jewish Folklore in Israel." *Jewish Folklore and Ethnology Review* 11: 1–2 (1989): 2–11.

Jaffe, N. *The Way Meat Loves Salt.* New York: Henry Holt, 1998.

Jones, Alison. *Larousse Dictionary of World Folklore.* New York: Larousse Kingfisher Chambers, 1996.

Koen-Sarano, Matilda. *Folktales of Joha, Jewish Trickster.* Translated by David Herman. Philadelphia: The Jewish Publication Society, 2003.
    King Solomon and the Golden Fish. Translated by Reginetta Haboucha. Detroit, MI: Wayne State University Press, 2004.

Levita, Shabbatia Carmuz. *Sepher Ha-Yashar.* Translated by Edgar J. Goodspeed. Boston: Beacon Press, 1933.

Lowney, Chris. *A Vanished World: Medieval Spain's Golden Age of Enlightenment.* New York: Simon & Shuster, 2005.

Mann, Stanley. *A Land of Pure Dreams.* Hagshama Department of World Zionist Organization. http://www.wzo.org.il/en/resources/view.asp?id=1472 (accessed December 3, 2005).

Noy, Dov, ed. *Folktales of Israel.* Chicago: University of Chicago Press, 1963.
    The Foundation Stone and Creation. Jerusalem: Valirushalayim, 1966.
    "The Jewish Versions of the 'Animal Languages' Folktale. (AT670): A Typological-Structural Study," *Scripta Hierosolymitana* 22 (1971): 171–208.

Ong, Walter. *Literacy and Orality.* Cambridge: Cambridge University Press, 1991.

Rapaport, A. S. *The Folklore of the Jews.* London, 1937.

Richmond, W. E., ed. *Studies in Folklore in Honor of Distinguished Services of Professor Stith Thompson.* Bloomington: Indiana University Press, 1991.

Schram, Peninnah. *Tales of Elijah the Prophet.* Northvale, NJ: Jason Aronson, 1991.

Schwartz, Howard. *Elijah's Violin and Other Jewish Fairy Tales.* New York: Harper & Row, 1983.

Schwarzwold, Ora. History of Ladino. http://www.jewish-languages.org/judeo-spanish.html (accessed September 15, 2005).

Sydow, Karl von. "Geograph and Folktale-Oicotypes." *Selected Papers on Folklore* (1948): 44–53.

Whiston, William. *Works of Flavius Josephus.* www.ccel.org/j/josephus/works/ant-19.html (accessed March 20, 2006).

Yassif, Eli. *Jewish Folklore: An Annotated Bibliography.* New York and London: Garland, 1986.

Glossary

alef: The first letter of the Hebrew alphabet.

Alef Bet: The Hebrew alphabet.

ARGAMAN: An amulet (good luck charm) representing five angels: Ariel, Raphael, Gabriel, Michael, and Nuriel.

Ashkenazim: Jews of Eastern Europe.

Baal Shem Tov: Another name for Rabbi Israel ben Eliezer (1698–1760), founder of Hasidism, a form of Judaism that emphasizes worship through singing and storytelling.

ben adam: A good person.

boreka: A cookie-like treat.

brit milah: Circumcision.

brusha: A bad witch.

djinn: A genie.

Et higi'ah: The time of singing has come (from The Song of Songs); time to return to Israel.

Eretz Yisra'el: Land of Israel.

hakham: A word sometimes used instead of "rabbi" to avoid confusion with an Arabic word, "rab," a name for God not to be applied to a human.

halakhah (pl. *halakhot):* Talmudic law, rules for Jews to live by.

ha-Shem: Literally, "the name." A respectful reference to God.

Havdalah: End of Sabbath service.

heder: Literally, "room." Historically, the small elementary school where Jewish boys met to study Talmud.

henna: An orange-colored dye used to color a bride's hands and feet.

iman: A Muslim religious ruler.

kenesa: House of prayer.

Magen David: Literally, "shield of David." The six-pointed Star of David.

mellah yahudi: A ghetto, a Jewish neighborhood.

midrash: Written interpretations and discussions of the laws, customs, and rituals of Jewish life mentioned in the Torah.

mikveh: A ritual bath.

mitzvah: A good deed, a blessing.

Qur'an: Holy book of Islam.

Shabbat: The Sabbath.

sofer: A scribe of the Torah.

soudades: A keepsake: the key to the home abandoned by a Jew from Spain or Portugal who fled from the Inquisition.

tallit: A prayer shawl.

Talmud: The collection of ancient rabbinic laws, commentaries, and traditions related to the Torah.

tav: The last letter of the Hebrew alphabet.

Torah: The first five books of the Bible.

tzadik: Literally, "righteous one." A wise or learned scholar.

tzitzit: Fringe affixed to the four corners of a tallit.

Tzohar: A glowing stone that holds the primordial light of creation.